Bad Blood

Krys Batts

The Real Ideal, LLC

Copyright © 2024 by Krys Batts

All rights reserved.

No portion of this book may be reproduced in any form without written permission from the publisher or author, except as permitted by U.S. copyright law.

With gratitude to Aunt Carolyn, an avid reader who made time to critique this novel as I wrote it.

It is what it is—or is it?

Chapter 1

The last three years had been hell on wheels for Fern Walker. It had been that long since her husband, Woody, had decided to quit his job as a manager at the local bowling alley. He'd said that he was fed up with customers cursing him out for one reason or another and he wasn't paid enough to endure it. The problem was that his meager salary was essential to paying their bills and keeping food on the table. And now that he'd chosen to take a permanent vacation, Fern was forced to work almost nonstop to feed five mouths, which included their three children. This was no easy feat on a waitress's income.

Since becoming the sole breadwinner in the household, Fern was so exhausted that she appeared comatose when asleep. Meanwhile, her waking hours were spent living her life on instant replay. At four o'clock each afternoon, she rolled out of bed and reported to work at Bernie's Bistro. After finishing the night shift, she went straight home to cook breakfast for the children before they left for school. Then she spent the next few hours doing laundry and tidying up the house as Woody played video games in the living room. By the time she hit the sack, her head was so heavy that she could barely think straight. And her eyes closed with sheer gratitude that she had made it through another day without losing her mind.

But this time, before she could nod off, her eyes flew back open. A bolt of anger surged through her like a raging wildfire. By God, she was as mad as a hornet! How could that lazy son of a gun watch her come and go without feeling ashamed? Had she been too good to him? Did he suddenly think that she was nothing more than a mule? They had been married for seventeen years, and he had spent the last three living like a bum—eating free food, using free water, and running up the electricity bill as if he were entitled to the comforts of a productive adult.

Time and again they had argued about Woody's sloth until she was blue in the face. But nothing—no placation, no insults, no tears—could move him. And this morning's altercation had been no different. The kids had been eating breakfast when Woody had ambled into the kitchen to scavenge for leftovers only to find all the pots empty. Wearing plaid pajama pants and a T-shirt that was two sizes too small, he could've been mistaken for a vagrant. "All the biscuits and gravy are gone?"

"I only made enough for the children." Fern was standing at the sink, washing the bowls and utensils she had used to cook the meal. She couldn't have cared less if Woody starved to death.

"What am I supposed to eat?"

"Get yourself some yogurt out of the refrigerator."

"I don't want yogurt. I want some real food. I want an omelet, bacon, and pancakes."

Fern rinsed a bowl without responding.

"Did you hear me?"

"Woody, I'm tired. If you don't want yogurt, then go buy something from McDonald's. Or go to your mama's house. I'm sure she'd be happy to cook something for you."

"So it's like that, huh?"

"It's been like that for a while."

"Hmph." He scratched his navel and walked over to their seventeen-year-old daughter, Cricket, who, like all three children, loved him as truly as the day was long. "I'm going to need your car tonight. I have some business to handle."

"Okay, D—"

"You can't take her car," Fern interjected with menace. "Go buy your own car if you need one so badly."

"Go buy this. Go buy that. You're meaner than the devil himself. I need the car, Fern."

"Cricket needs it, too."

"She doesn't mind if I use it. Do you, baby?"

"Well—"

"It doesn't matter if she minds. I mind, and I said no." Fern hoped that putting her foot down wouldn't start World War III. Under her unwavering glare, Woody got an apple from a bowl of fruit at the center of the table and bit into it. He and Fern then held a Mexican standoff with their dirty looks before he shuffled out of the kitchen. Minutes later, she heard the front door open and close as he left the house without telling anyone where he was going.

She was glad that he was gone. She thought that she'd get better rest without the muffled sound of Pokémon coming through the wall. But she couldn't fall asleep. Instead, she lay in bed reliving the years that had brought them to this point, where Woody was perfectly content to be an irresponsible dolt. Unsurprisingly, the stress of carrying the full load had taken its toll on Fern. Her body was shaped liked a pear, her rust-colored hair was turning gray, and her legs looked more like totem poles. At age thirty-six, she was nowhere close to the head turner that she once was. And she was almost certain that Woody was seeing another woman while she was at work. She wished that he would just move in with the floozy. Fern would gladly be rid of him. But maybe his side piece was too smart for that. Maybe she was using him for something, although Fern couldn't imagine what that might be. He was terrible in bed and packed a beer belly that was heavy enough to suffocate any woman who dared to lie under him. Not to mention he was usually broke since Fern had removed his name from her bank accounts. Whatever was going on between them, it seemed that the mistress wasn't dumb enough to hitch her wagon to a black hole.

"I don't understand why you put up with him," her sister, Jasmine, regularly fussed. "You don't need or love him. Put him out already."

"The kids love him." Fern always used the kids as her excuse for keeping Woody around. It was easier than booting him. "Anyway, you're not married. So you don't understand the position that I'm in."

"I don't have to be married to understand that you're letting a man take advantage of you. It's not the example you should be setting for your kids."

"Don't you worry about my kids. They're not your business."

"They're all of our business. And if you're not careful, you're going to force Daddy's hand. I heard him talking about getting his gun the other day."

"Getting his gun for what?"

"You know what. Ever since Woody slapped you last year, Daddy's been waiting to get even with him."

"Daddy will do no such thing. I've already told him to let me handle Woody my way."

"He's not listening to you. He's going to do what he believes is best for his family."

"I'm already doing what's best. I'll talk to Daddy." Fern knew that her father could be stubborn, but he needed to stop talking about knocking off her husband. The whole family had gotten wind of his threat, and she worried that he might mean business. She wasn't stupid. She knew that Woody had to go. But knowing it and doing something about it were two different things. And as things stood, Fern had no shortage of things to do. She'd eventually get around to Woody, but she wasn't looking forward to the hassle he would surely put her through.

"What'll it be tonight, Lionel? Same as usual?"

A retired army veteran, Lionel was one of the restaurant's regulars and a sage penny-pincher. As he perused the menu, Fern stood ready to log his order in a computerized tablet. She would've preferred to use a little pad and pen, as was once customary, but the owner, Bernie, insisted that automating the orders would speed everything up. He wanted as many butts in and out of the seats as possible.

Despite appearing to consider the options, Lionel always ordered a grilled cheese sandwich and tomato soup. "Tell me, Fern, is the meatloaf any good?"

"It's a customer favorite, so it must be. Do you wanna try it?"

"What would it cost with my veteran and senior discounts?"

"Oh, I don't know. Maybe around five bucks and change."

He paused to think about her estimate. "I think I'll get the grilled cheese and fries." He folded the menu and set it down.

"No tomato soup?"

"I want the tomato soup, too."

"You sure about that? I don't think that you could eat it all."

"You're right. Scratch the fries. I'll just get the tomato soup."

"All right. Good choice." Fern punched the order into the tablet. "I'll bring it out as soon as it's ready."

"Thank you, Fern." He leaned a little closer to her and lowered his voice. "Where's Sharon? I was hoping she'd be here tonight."

"I'm covering for her. Her kid is sick, so she stayed home."

"That's too bad. I hope he feels better soon."

"He'll be fine. I thought you would've asked her out by now."

"You know as well as I do that nobody wants an old geezer like me. And I wouldn't know what to do with her anyway.

She's still a young gal, and my body ain't what it used to be, if you know what I mean."

"I know exactly what you mean." Fern peered behind his booth through the window. It was only six o'clock, but the sky was already pitch-black. She hated the winter months in Texas. One of these days, she was going to pack up and leave Luna for somewhere like California or Florida. And she'd live in a big city, where it wasn't so easy for everyone to stay in each other's business.

A tap on her shoulder interrupted her thoughts.

"Fern, you've got a call," Jared, a fellow waiter, had come to tell her.

"Is it one of my kids?"

"Naw, it's Woody. Do you want me to take a message?"

"No, lemme find out what the heck he wants." She looked back at Lionel. "Your order will be out in no time, sweetie."

"You're the best." He smiled wryly as Fern walked to the back to take Woody's call.

"Yeah, what is it?"

"I wanna know why you told Cricket that she could drive to the football game tonight. You know good and well that I need the car."

She should've known that he had called to squabble. "Have you lost your mind? We already had this conversation this morning. And I'm telling you again that if you need a car, get a job and buy one yourself."

"We both helped Cricket buy that car. She put up half the money, and we paid the other half. So it's half my car, and I need it tonight."

"You didn't contribute one dime to that car, you lazy—" She stopped short, realizing that she was speaking too loudly. The last thing she needed was to let this jackass get her fired. She glanced around furtively to see if she had drawn attention to herself.

"What's yours is mine, Fern. Now, you may not like that, but that's the way it is. So any money you used to help buy the car was my money, too. And that technically makes the car half mine."

"The car is all hers. Her name is the only one on the title. I made sure of that."

"Well, my name is on the deed to our house. And as long as she's living under my roof, I have a right to use the car. I've asked Calvin to pick me up so I can go get it. He's on his way right now."

Fern hit the ceiling. If she could've gone through the phone and strangled him at that moment, she'd be rightly charged with murder. "You'd better call Calvin back and tell him not to bother. You are not taking that car."

"Oh, yes I am. But don't worry, Fern. I'll make sure one of her friends can bring her home after the game."

"You listen to me," she hissed, "and you listen real good. If I find out that you took Cricket's car, it'll be the last time you're around to take anything from anyone else. You got me?"

"All I hear is blah, blah, blah. I'll see you in the morning, darlin'."

Woody hung up as Fern shouted more threats into the phone. She was calling him back when Jared rushed over to her.

"Hey, is everything all right?"

"No, everything is not all right." She clenched her teeth as the phone rang at her house. "I swear to God that I'm going to kill that man. Mark my words, Jared, I'm going to kill him."

"What happened this time?"

"Hang on." She turned from Jared to speak with her fourteen-year-old daughter, Hope, who had answered the phone. "Baby, put your daddy on the phone. I need to speak with him."

"He just left with Calvin."

"He did? That son of a—"

"Shh." Jared cautioned Fern to keep her voice down.

Heeding his warning, she chewed her lip for a second. "If he comes back home before I do, tell him to call me. Okay?"

"Okay, Mama."

Fern hung up the phone and stared at it, her thoughts racing as she pictured Cricket helplessly handing her car keys over to Woody. She knew what she had to do. "Jared, I need to leave, and I don't know if I'll be back tonight."

"Gail can probably fill in for you. She doesn't have any plans."

"That'll be good." Fern removed her apron and rushed to her locker for her purse. She then looked for Carlos, the night manager, but he was in the bathroom. "When Carlos come out, tell him that I had a family emergency, okay?"

"Okay. And don't worry. I'll take care of Lionel."

"Thank you." She dashed past Lionel as Jared approached his table. Soon, she was in her car and speeding away from the diner.

When Fern reached the football game, she hurriedly parked her car and scampered to the stadium entrance, hoping she had arrived in time to head off Woody. But at the sight of Cricket standing with a group of friends, her pace slowed. She was too late, and Cricket's obvious dejection was heartbreaking.

"Daddy just took my car," she unhappily informed Fern. Wearing black leggings and a simple tunic top, she looked as cute as a button despite her drooping lips.

"I know, and I'm sorry about that."

Each of Cricket's friends greeted Fern before one named Aden said, "Mr. Walker was in a real hurry."

"How long has he been gone?"

"Around five minutes. We came outside the stadium so Cricket could show him where the car was parked. And he left as soon as he got the keys."

"Did he say where he was going?"

"No," Cricket grumbled. "He just said that he needed the car and to call you if I need a ride home."

Fern could only shake her head with disgust. Woody was easily the sorriest excuse for a man that she had ever known. He hadn't always been this way, but something had snapped when he quit his job. Behind them, an excited cheer went up in the stadium.

"Do you need me to come back for you after the game? You can have my cell phone and call me when you're ready." Ideally, Cricket would have her own mobile phone, but Fern's income couldn't be stretched that far.

"No, that's okay, Mama. Aden's going to bring me home."

"Yeah, I've got her back, Mrs. Walker."

"Okay, thank you. I appreciate that." There was nothing more that Fern could do. "You kids go on back inside the stadium and enjoy the game."

"Are you going back to work, Mama?"

"I don't know. Maybe not. I'm thinking about taking the rest of the night off." Although she needed the money, there were more pressing matters to address tonight. Fern slowly walked to her car while ruminating on Woody's selfish actions. He had finally pushed her to the limit, and she would be waiting to issue his walking papers when he got home.

That night, Fern fell asleep in front of the television, and woke up to a kid show about animal wildlife. Other than that, the house was quiet since everyone slept in on Saturdays. She hadn't heard either Cricket or Woody come in and so checked her daughter's bedroom before looking for Woody in theirs. As expected, Cricket was sound asleep, but there were no signs of Woody. That was very odd.

Fern went to a window to see if Cricket's car was in the driveway, but it was nowhere in sight. "Where has that man gotten himself to?" He probably had lost track of time at his mistress's home. Fern would've been jumping for joy if he didn't have Cricket's car.

Electing to put off errands until Woody came back, she started cooking breakfast for the kids. Her youngest, Thad, would be waking up soon with an appetite that rivaled Godzilla's. As the bacon fried, Hope wandered into the kitchen wiping sleep from her eyes.

"Hey, Mama."

"Hey yourself. Did you sleep well?"

"Not really. Cricket was mad at Daddy for taking her car and wouldn't stop talking about it for most of the night."

"He shouldn't have done that. I'm waiting for him to get home so we can discuss it." Fern kept her more explicit thoughts to herself, not wanting to be one of those women who bash their children's father while in their company. "You hungry?"

"Yeah."

"Well, get yourself a plate. Breakfast is almost ready."

"Okay." Hope went to a cabinet and stood on her tippy-toes to reach the plates. Although on the short side, she was the most athletic of the kids and could climb up trees and fences faster than a squirrel. "Are you coming to my soccer game today? Or do you have to work?"

"Lord, I forgot about the game." Fern removed the bacon from the pan and placed it atop paper towels so that the grease could be absorbed. "What time does it start?"

"Three o'clock."

Fern sighed. "I was thinking about picking up another shift today since I left work early last night."

"If Daddy doesn't come back with Cricket's car, I'm going to need you to take me."

"He should be back any minute now."

"What if he's not?"

"If he's not, I'll call Stacy's parents and ask if they can take you to the game with them."

"But I want you to come."

"I know, honey, but I can't make it today. Maybe next weekend, though."

"You said that last weekend."

"And I meant it last weekend. But something's come up, and I can't do it, much as I'd like to." Fern scraped a helping of scrambled eggs onto her daughter's plate along with grits and bacon. "You eat up. And don't worry about the soccer game. I'll make sure you get there on time."

"All right." Hope frowned unhappily while picking up a strip of bacon.

By one o'clock, Woody still had not come back home, and Fern was starting to get a little worried—not about his welfare, but about Cricket's car. So she called his mother, praying that she knew something about his whereabouts. "Hi, Liddie. Have you heard from Woody today?"

"No, of course not. Woody only calls me on Sundays. Why?"

"He took Cricket's car last night, and he hasn't come back home yet. I was hoping that maybe he was with you."

"Can't say that he is. Have you tried Roy or Calvin? You know how they are, three peas in a pod."

"I hadn't thought about that, but I'll call them now."

"If I hear from him, I'll let you know."

"I'd appreciate it. Thank you."

Fern's next call was to Stacy's house to confirm that her father could give Hope a ride to her soccer game. She then called both Calvin and Roy. Neither of them had heard from Woody since last night. And Calvin claimed to have no knowledge of where Woody had gone after hijacking Cricket's car.

"For the love of God!" Fern was beginning to think that Woody had wrecked the car and was stranded somewhere without access to a phone. He could be anywhere. And the car could be damaged beyond repair.

Preparing for the worst, she changed into her work uniform. Before leaving, she gave the kids instructions to call her as soon as they saw or heard from Woody.

"I don't have the money to replace Cricket's car," Fern confided to her coworker Deedee while waiting for the cooks to complete her customers' orders. "I spent every last dime of my savings to replace our AC unit last month."

"The car is insured, ain't it?" Deedee grabbed the plates of food that must be delivered to her tables. She was a tiny, dark-haired woman with one child and a husband who actually held down a job. She couldn't possibly understand the financial jam that Fern was in.

"It's only covered for liability. I couldn't afford full coverage for a seventeen-year-old."

"Oh no." She expertly balanced the plates between her hands and wrists. "Maybe you can get a loan for another car."

"That's not an option. I'd go bankrupt trying to pay it. And anyway, Woody messed up my credit. I couldn't finance a paper clip right now."

"That man is more trouble than he's worth."

"Tell me about it."

Deedee scuddled to deliver the plates of food as Fern stressed about all the problems she faced if Cricket's car was undriveable. She relied on Cricket's help to get Thad and Hope to their sporting events. Without that car...She didn't want to think about it anymore. She had to wait for Woody to come home and try not to give herself a heart attack in the process.

"Damn shame that a grown man is so irresponsible." Deedee had come back just as the orders for one of Fern's tables was being set beneath the heating lamps. "I got my first job when I was sixteen, and I've been working ever since. I know you don't want Cricket to work, but—"

"No, she needs to enjoy herself as long as she can. I don't mind if she works during the summer like she did this year, but not while she's got school and homework. She'll have the rest of her life to work and pay bills once she's an adult." Fern began to place the plates on a large tray that she would use to carry them.

"That's true, but I'm sure she can get a part-time job and still enjoy her life, Fern. She could pay for her own car, and you wouldn't be so worried about every little thing. You're killing yourself for no reason."

"I'm not killing myself. But I've got half a mind to kill Woody. It would be one less mouth to feed." She carried the tray to her customers and set their respective plates before them. "Is there anything else that I can get y'all?"

"Can we get a bottle of ketchup please?" Out of the four patrons, only one—a freckled redhead—spoke up. "And some extra napkins?"

"Sure, coming right up. Anything else?"

The redhead looked at everyone else around the table before answering. "No, ma'am. That'll be all."

"Great."

Fern walked to a nearby dolly to retrieve the items, thinking more about Woody's gall than what was in front of her. She didn't see Deedee coming her way with a load of hot plates until they collided. Suddenly, the sound of breaking glass and shrieks filled the restaurant as Fern and Deedee reacted to the mess that was now splattered across the floor. They both knelt and began to clean it up as Bernie came running.

"What happened?"

"I'm sorry, Bernie," Deedee said while gathering up the broken dishware. "I was a little clumsy, and I must've tripped while I was carrying the food."

"That's not what happened," Fern gloomily admitted.

"Yes, it is." Deedee looked up at Bernie. "I'm sorry. I'll have this cleaned up in no time."

"I'll tell Winston to come help you. Fern, you've got orders up and ready to go."

"Okay, thank you, Bernie."

She and Deedee exchanged looks as Bernie walked away. They both knew that the cost of the food on the floor was going to come out of Deedee's paycheck.

"Thank you, Deedee. You didn't have to do that."

"I don't mind. You have enough problems to think about."

Fern lowered her eyes with shame and stood up. She hated being so financially strapped. It was so bad that even thirty dollars of wasted food could set her back if it was deducted from her check. Tears blurred her vision as she walked away to retrieve the orders. When she returned to the dining area, the lady waiting for ketchup and napkins reminded her, unwittingly causing Fern to choke up. She managed a timid apology before swiftly fulfilling all of her customers' requests. Afterward, she rushed into the bathroom and bawled, her eyes turning into beady, bloodshot slits. Her life was not supposed to be like this. She was supposed to be a happily married housewife, a soccer mom, something that suggested having plenty of money in the bank. Instead, she had gotten stuck with a worthless husband and an economic status that was barely above poverty. And where was he while she toiled to support their family? Out joyriding in his daughter's car? Sleeping off a hangover somewhere? Maybe rolling in the hay with his mistress? Her self-pity was replaced with anger at these thoughts. The tears instantly dried up, and she washed her face with cold water to reduce the swelling beneath her eyes. A quick once-over revealed that her effort was pointless. She looked lousy, but she couldn't let that stop her. She still had customers to take care of and money to earn.

She exited the bathroom, checked on all her customers, and then called her kids to find out if Woody had come home. Unfortunately, he was still MIA. If no one heard from him by tomorrow, she was going to report that Cricket's car had been stolen. Woody had managed to live free of charge, but Fern would be damned if he was also going to get a free car.

Chapter 2

Pat Dupree was a Massachusetts native who had settled down in Luna with his college sweetheart, Ellie, over thirty years ago. Together, they had raised five beautiful, headstrong children, and were now empty nesters with retirement fast approaching. For his part, Pat could hardly wait to hang up his hat and gun as the town's sheriff. His knees had lately started talking back in a bad way, and he was dog-tired of running down illegal immigrants who crossed over from a neighboring town in Mexico. Most of the time, they came in search of work or to visit family members, which Pat had no problem with. But the law was the law, and he had busted both knees during chases on foot to enforce it. Now he was ready to do more of what he wanted to do—fishing and reading.

That morning, he sat at his desk with his boots resting on a corner, absentmindedly picking his teeth with a toothpick. Luna had always been a fairly quiet place with very little crime. The residents all knew each other, and many families slept with their doors unlocked. If the Mexico border weren't so close, Pat wouldn't have anything to do—and wouldn't that be grand. As it was, there was no need for a large police force. The community was satisfied that Pat and his five deputies had everything under control.

"Pat, you've got a call on line one." The station's phone operator, Dottie, stood in his doorway. She was in her sixties and wore her silver hair in a feathered style that kicked sand at her age.

"Who is it?"

"Liddie Walker. She says that her son, Woody, is missing."

He swung his feet to the floor. "For how long?"

"Going on two days."

"Aw, hell. That's nothing. He probably got drunk and fell in a ditch somewhere. He'll wake up and go home soon."

"He's more of a gamer than a drunk, Sheriff."

"Then he's probably holed up playing video games with somebody. He's got nothing better to do, last I heard."

"I'm not disagreeing with you, but Liddie still needs to talk to you."

"All right, I'll take the call." He placed his hand on the phone receiver, knowing that he would need to muster more patience than he felt. "Good morning, Liddie. How can I help you?"

"Good morning, Sheriff. I'm calling because Woody has been gone for two days without a word to anyone. It's not like him, and I'm worried."

"Yes, I understand your concern. Have you spoken to Fern? She ought to know where he is."

"I just spoke with her before I called you. She has no idea."

"She hasn't called us, so I assume that she's not worried. Maybe you should give it another day or two, see if he turns up."

"Sheriff, my son has called me every Sunday for years. I'm embarrassed to admit it, but he's had a very hard time finding work. So I've been giving him a little money to help out."

That explained how Woody paid for bourbon shots at the local bar. Everyone knew that Fern had cut him off. "But he didn't call you yesterday."

"That's right."

"Did you already try Calvin and Roy?"

"I didn't, but Fern did."

"And they don't know where he is?"

"No."

Pat rubbed his chin. The more he heard, the more he agreed with Liddie that something strange was afoot. But he didn't yet see a need to open a missing person case. "He's a grown man, Liddie. I don't want to jump the gun here and go looking for someone who doesn't want to be found. I really do think he'll show up when he's ready. You just said that he's been struggling to find a job. Maybe he needs some time alone to think about things."

Liddie huffed. "My son? We're talking about Woody, Sheriff. I love him, but I'm not oblivious to his shortcomings. If he hasn't gone home for two days, then something is wrong, very wrong."

She was right, of course. He knew Woody, and there weren't many places he could be since he was low on cash. And his boneheaded conversation limited the number of people who could tolerate his company for more than a few minutes. "Okay, Liddie. You win. I'll start asking around and see what I can find out."

"Thank you. Please call me when you've got some news."

"I will. You can count on it."

"Sheriff." Dottie reappeared before he hung up the phone. "You've got Fern on line two."

"I guess we already know why." He switched the extension to line two. "Hello, Fern. I just finished talking to Liddie. I'm sorry to hear that Woody is missing. How are you holding up?"

"I'm doing my best. I didn't know she was going to call you."

"Well, she did. And I'm glad that you called because I need to speak with you, even though I honestly don't think that there's any cause for alarm."

"That's good to know, but I didn't call to discuss Woody. I called because Cricket's car was stolen."

Pat immediately straightened with surprise. "Really? When?"

"Two days ago."

"Two days ago? Why didn't you or Cricket call me sooner?"

"Because we hoped that Woody would bring it back."

"Wait, hold on a second. You're calling to report that Woody stole Cricket's car?"

"That's right. Her name is the only one on the title, and he took the car against her will."

"So you know for a fact that Woody has the car?"

"Yes, I do. Cricket watched him drive off in it."

"Two days ago."

"Right."

He again rubbed his chin. This whole thing was getting stranger by the minute. "Tell me something, Fern. Are you worried about Woody at all? Or just the car?"

"We need the car, Sheriff."

"And what about Woody?"

"What about him?"

Her callous response raised the hairs on the back of his neck. He had long expected Fern to send Woody packing, but had she gone ballistic and done something drastic? "When was the last time you saw him?"

"Before I left for work on Friday night."

"What sort of mood was he in? Was he upset about anything?"

"Not that I know of."

"Did he say that he was going somewhere?"

"Woody doesn't tell me much, Sheriff. He likes to play video games when he's at home. When he's not here, I don't know what he does with himself."

Fern's indifference led Pat to withhold the rest of his questions until he could speak with her in person. He wanted to observe her body language when she answered them. "I need to come by and take a look around for anything that might help us find Woody. Would that be all right with you?"

"I don't know what good that'll do, but you're more than welcome to come. Are you going to look for the car, too?"

"Yes, absolutely. But it sounds like finding Woody would also mean finding the car."

"If he still has it. You know he's broke, Sheriff. He could've tried to sell it illegally or something. You can't put anything past that man."

"I'll put out BOLOs for both Woody and the car."

"Separately?"

"Yes." He pulled out a pen and pad. "Give me the information about the car." He wrote down the details necessary to locate it. "Also, do you happen to know what Woody was wearing when he disappeared with Cricket's car?"

"No, but I'm sure Cricket can tell you."

"All right. She's at school today?"

"Yes, she should be home by four thirty or five."

He made a note to speak with Cricket later. "And what about a cell phone? What's his number?"

"He doesn't have one."

"That's too bad. We could've used it to track him." The options for easily locating Woody had just been obliterated. "I'll share what we know so far with my deputies."

"Okay, thank you."

"And I should be at your house in around thirty minutes."

"Sure, and I'd appreciate it if you'd come and go quickly. I haven't slept yet, and I need to rest before going to work this evening."

"I'll make it as fast as I can."

"Great. I'll see you soon, Sheriff."

He slowly placed the phone receiver in its cradle and sat in silence for a few minutes, mulling over his suspicions. He hoped that he was wrong, but he had to consider the real possibility that Fern had—to put it lightly—dispatched Woody. And now she could be using the car to cover her tracks, pretending that she didn't already know that he would be found dead in it. The good Lord knew that Woody had it coming. But if Pat found evidence that Fern had committed murder, he would have no choice but to arrest her. No matter how much he liked her, the law was the law. And he would enforce it regardless of how he felt about it.

When Pat stepped into Fern's house, the first thing he noticed was the tangy aroma of Italian food. "Something sure does smell good in here." He hadn't eaten lunch yet, and his stomach growled as he closed the front door behind himself.

"I'm cooking spaghetti. I always make sure the kids have a decent meal waiting for them when they get home from school."

"You're a great mother. There's not many left like you." His eyes roamed the living room where they were standing.

"Can I get you something to drink? A glass of water or tea?"

"Water would be nice. Thank you."

Fern hastened to the kitchen as Pat began to walk around the room. He noticed an array of magazines lying atop the coffee table and thumbed through a few. Most were dedicated to hair, makeup, and clothes—stuff that young girls were usually obsessed with. His eyes then fell on an Xbox controller. He had never been interested in video games, but his sons had been addicted to them. He picked it up and turned it around, inspecting all of the buttons on it. It looked like the most recent version had doodads that hadn't been on the ones his kids had used.

"That's Woody's favorite object in the house," Fern said as she returned with Pat's water and handed it to him.

"Thank you." He set down the controller. "I can't say that I've ever understood why people like video games so much. I always preferred playing football when I was growing up."

"I've said the same thing for years. Thank goodness Thad loves soccer. I couldn't stand the idea of him being like his father."

Pat was well aware of Fern's sentiments about Woody but had dismissed them until today. "How acrimonious is your relationship with him?"

"If we're talking, then we're arguing, Sheriff. It's best that he stay in his corner and I stay in mine."

He began to walk around the room again, looking for anything that seemed unusual or out of place. Nothing seemed awry. "Since you two don't get along, where does he sleep?"

"In our bedroom, of course."

He had expected Fern to say that he slept on the couch. "Can I look around the bedroom?"

"Knock yourself out."

He followed her to the bedroom, and she turned on the light. As with the living room, the space was spic and span.

Maybe too spic and span. "Does Woody have a notebook? Or has he been reading any books or magazines recently?"

Fern crossed her arms and leaned against the doorjamb. "He doesn't like to read or write. So, no, he doesn't have books of any kind around here."

Pat walked around the bed, staring at the carpet for any signs of blood splotches. Then he got down on his knees to look under the bed, where he saw a single shoebox. He grabbed it and stood back up so that Fern could see it. "Do you know what's in here?"

She looked dumbfounded and came closer. "I've never seen it before. That was under the bed?"

"Yeah. Do I have your permission to look inside?"

"Sure."

He lifted the lid and peered at the contents. There were at least fifty small, plastic packets of yellow pills. Surprised, he emptied one of the packets into his palm. "Is Woody on drugs?"

"No. I mean, I don't think so."

He watched her facial expression and then looked at her hands. No obvious signs of deception accompanied or followed her response. She seemed to be genuinely as shocked as he was. "You've never seen this box before?" He again watched her closely.

"No." She shook her head and reached for the pills, but he moved his hand away. "What do you think they are?"

"I don't know. I've never seen any that look like these." To help see any distinct markings, he held one up to the light. "Is it possible that they belong to one of your kids?"

"Hell no! I raised good kids. You won't find any better."

Pat focused a skeptical eye on Fern. "You sure about that? Kids can be pretty sneaky. That's their nature."

"Not my kids, no, sir. I rebuke that in the name of Jesus." She placed a palm on her chest and made the sign of the cross.

Pat had never known Fern to be a churchgoing woman, so her sudden attack of religion almost made him laugh. "I'd like to check their rooms."

"I have no problem with that. I know my kids, and you're not going to find any drugs."

He replaced the lid on the shoebox and carried it with him as he inspected each additional room. True to Fern's declaration, there were no drugs. However, Cricket had hidden several condoms under her mattress.

"Oh, my Lord!" Fern became faint and began gasping for air when Pat held up the condoms. "What is she doing with those?"

"If I have to explain that to you—"

"Oh, my Lord! No, God, no! Not my baby. I've talked to her about boys! I've told her how conniving they can be."

"It's not the end of the world, Fern."

"It is the end, especially if she gets pregnant!" She grabbed the condoms from Pat and stuffed them into a pocket on her skirt. "If I hadn't gotten pregnant at such a young age, I would've left this town and made something of myself. I don't want my girls to make the same mistakes that I did."

Pat was sorry that he had exposed Cricket's secret. He could see that Fern was not equipped to handle the situation. "If she's using condoms, then you don't need to worry about that." He wanted to reassure her, but—more than that—he wanted to leave.

"But what if the condom comes off? Or what if it has a hole in it? Then what? I'm not raising any more babies, Sheriff."

She was working herself into a frenzy, and Pat felt obligated to calm her down, to spare Cricket her mother's frantic rants.

He ushered Fern back into the living room and sat down with her, still keeping the shoebox close. "I'm going to talk to you as the parent of five grown children, Fern. And I don't mind saying that all five are doing well for themselves, but they all made different mistakes when they were younger. There's no avoiding that. I don't care how great a parent is."

"You and Ellie are excellent parents," she croaked. "You worked as a team to bring up those kids with good heads on their shoulders."

"That's true. We did."

"Well, I don't have that kind of partnership, Sheriff. I may as well be a single parent. Woody doesn't care about our children. He's never tried to teach them morals and ethics. And he's a terrible example for them, which I constantly have to hear about from everyone in my family."

Without knowing it, Fern had just created a list of suspects in Pat's mind, people who he would need to speak with about Woody's disappearance. He already knew that Fern's family hated Woody's guts. But if they were complaining about him on a regular basis, then someone could've finally done something about it. Pat tried to slyly delve a little deeper into Fern's last statement. "Do you know if anyone is mad enough at Woody to wanna hurt him?"

"I know plenty of people who have talked about teaching him a lesson, but that's just talk. You know how people are when they get mad. Heck, I've thought about strangling him myself more than a few times."

"So you don't think that there are any serious threats on his life?"

She paused and began to tap her foot. It was a sure sign that she was about to lie to him. "No, not that I know of." She continued to tap her foot for a few more seconds.

"Now, Fern, if you know something that you're not telling me, it won't be good for Woody. And I'm sure that you don't want any harm to come to the father of your children." Actually, he was sure of no such thing. But he hadn't seen anything around the house that suggested foul play, and his investigation would be a lot easier to carry out if Fern continued to trust him.

"I've told you all I know." She sighed sadly. "Did you know that Cricket is sexually active?"

"No." Pat didn't want to get pulled back into that discussion, but he saw no tactful way out of it. "I hadn't heard anything about it. And she may not be doing anything at all. Maybe she has the condoms because she's thinking about it. She's at that age where she's probably curious, probably thinks that she's met someone special."

"She's never mentioned anyone to me. And I thought that we were close enough to talk about everything."

"Then maybe she's not doing anything that you need to be concerned about."

"If she was your daughter, what would you do? I could use your advice because I'm coming up with nothing."

"You might not like my answer because I'd put the condoms back under her mattress without a word to her."

"Are you crazy? I asked for advice, not ruination."

"And I'm giving you my advice. Put the condoms back under the mattress, and let Cricket come to you if she wants to talk about whatever is going on. Otherwise, she's going to think you've been snooping around her room, and she won't trust you anymore."

"But I'm not the one who found the condoms. You did. You were the one snooping around her room."

"Yes, with your permission. But Cricket doesn't need to know that I found the condoms. Put them back where they were. That's my advice."

Fern pulled the condoms from her pocket and sighed again. "You're right. I don't like that answer. But it's the best advice that I'm going to get so I'll take it."

"Good." They both stood. "I'm going to send these pills to a lab so we can get them analyzed."

"You think that they might be behind Woody's disappearance?"

"Don't know. But it's the only lead that I've got so far." They walked toward the front door. "Hopefully, Woody will turn up soon."

"The only thing I'm worried about is Cricket's car."

Her persistent lack of concern for Woody continued to bother Pat. "We're looking for it." He exited the house and headed for his patrol car. "Let Cricket know that I'll be back when she gets home from school. I need to know whatever she can tell me about the last time she saw Woody."

"All right."

Fern closed the door as Pat got into his car and started the engine. He felt in his gut that Fern was somehow involved with Woody's disappearance. But her house didn't seem to be the scene of the crime. He needed to speak with Woody's closest friends, Calvin and Roy, next. They might have some intel that pointed his investigation in the right direction.

Chapter 3

Boone Jenkins—more commonly known as B.J.—was a gambling man with a modest record of success that he kept to himself. As luck would have it, he had a family full of moochers who would have no problem asking for handouts if they ever got wind of him having one spare dime. And though he'd left most of them behind in Alabama by joining the Marines and then retiring in Oklahoma, he knew that they kept their ears to the ground, which was a healthy incentive for him to refrain from jaw-jacking.

To look at him, one would think that he was the bullying type with a chip on his shoulder. At forty-three years old, he had a powerhouse build similar to a heavyweight fighter and typically wore a Yankees baseball cap that had long since seen its glory days. After leaving the military, he'd shrugged off shaving and ironing, which resulted in him looking rugged and at times unkempt. But this didn't matter since he didn't need to impress anyone. Aside from his elderly father, Joe, a good-hearted softy who'd moved in with him, B.J. didn't spend much time with people, being a loner and, as such, not caring for their company.

He'd been prepared to ride out the rest of life hunting deer and living off the land, but his plans had gone sideways when Joe had suffered a stroke last year. The subsequent medical bills had shot a titanic hole through B.J.'s budget, which was tailored to manage only their basic needs. There was no way in hell that his retirement checks could be spread out enough to pay off the medical bills that Medicare didn't cover, a shortfall that had forced B.J. to scramble for a way to supplement his income.

His initial campaign had landed him in a club bouncer job, which hadn't gone too well. He was short on patience with the knuckleheads who patronized the establishment and had nearly broken a customer's arm when he wouldn't leave a lady alone. He'd been fired immediately, but the experience had given him clarity on what he did and didn't want. He did not want a job that required him to get on with a lot of people. He did want a legal means to earn money as easily as possible. As these preferences greatly reduced his options, he eventually wound up trying online gambling, which in no way guaranteed a reliable stipend. But it was what it was.

Being a simple man, B.J. preferred to keep things simple. So he started out with bubblegum wagers like slots and table games, but he inevitably spent more money than he won. With lowered spirits, he then joined a few chatrooms and learned that some people were cashing in big bets placed on video gaming websites, particularly those dedicated to something called Pokémon. They shared a few tips that B.J. immediately tested on his own gambles. Soon he was winning enough money to make extra payments on his father's medical bills. But these results were not the windfall that B.J. wanted. His ultimate goal was to get out from under the debt altogether—and this got him to thinking. There was clearly a huge demand for these games, and people were willing to pay good money to play them. So why shouldn't he launch his own video game? It might take a little while to get it done, but he could see a real opportunity for financial freedom. The only drawback was that B.J. had no interest in playing video games, much less designing one. But he already knew who he would tap for the expertise that he lacked—a guy named Woody Walker. B.J. had been following him on the Pokémon website and had placed several bets on Woody's winning probabilities. Most of the time, the bets had paid off, giving B.J. the impression that Woody's knowledge about Pokémon would be perfect for designing a new game that was equally appealing. In return for sharing his insights and recommendations, B.J. would gladly pay him a one-time fee, the key being one-time because B.J. had no intention of sharing ownership of the game.

Stoked about his ingenious idea, he'd contacted Woody through the website's private chatroom and asked if they could meet to discuss his proposal. Later that same week, he'd made a round-trip visit to Luna solely for the purpose of looking Woody in the eyes as they forged an agreement. Prior to their meeting, B.J. had never been to Luna, let alone heard of the town. It was barely a dot on the map, so small that a person could drive straight through it in one blink of an eye.

He remembered sitting across from Woody at a truck stop that served breakfast on the outskirts of town. Woody was not at all what B.J. had expected. Instead of a twentysomething nerd, he was borderline obese, maybe a tad younger than B.J., and obviously uncomfortable under his gaze. He looked like a man who needed money worse than B.J. did. He looked like a man who shouldn't have so much time on his hands to play video games. But then B.J. reminded himself that he, too, was disheveled. It was very possible that Woody was equally as surprised by B.J.'s appearance. Neither man could accurately judge the other if looks were going to be the measure.

"Woody, it's a pleasure to put a face to the name." B.J. reached across the table and shook his hand.

"Same here." Woody grinned without showing his teeth and then reached for a menu that was on the table. "My wife was too tired to make breakfast this morning, so I think I'll grab something while we're here."

"You're married? I didn't expect that."

"Why not?"

"Because you have time to play video games. You must not have any kids."

"We have three." Woody didn't share additional details like the kids' ages or sexes. Nor did B.J. inquire further. "Say, are you paying since you asked for this meeting?"

The question solidified B.J.'s assumptions. Woody was strapped for money. He had to be because no man with even a few bucks in his wallet would expect another man to buy his meal. This raised a minor red flag for B.J., but he allowed the greed he criticized in others to overtake his good sense. Hooked on the promise of dollar signs, he agreed to pay the bill. "Sure, that's fine. Get what you want."

"Great." Woody looked like a kid in a toy store as he proceeded to order everything he could stuff in his face.

This rude lack of restraint said a great deal about his character, and B.J. began to more deeply assess how much money to offer Woody for his assistance. He had initially been thinking about paying him five grand, but the price was rapidly plummeting.

Without telling Woody much about himself, B.J. explained his interest in creating a video game and paying Woody for consulting services. The way Woody's eyes popped out told B.J. that he would readily accept two grand, which was the fee they agreed on. "I'm glad that we were able to hammer this out so quickly. I'll just have my lawyer draw up the paperwork and send it to you later this week."

"What about the money?"

Woody was so fixated on getting paid that B.J. wished he'd offered him a thousand dollars. He wondered what Woody did with the money he must surely be winning from playing Pokémon. He could only assume that with a wife and three kids, the lion's share must be going to his family's living expenses.

"After you sign the contract, I'll wire half the payment to you. Then, once your services have been rendered, I'll wire the other half to you. Does that work?"

"It sure does." This time when Woody smiled, he showed his teeth, which were stained yellow as though they hadn't been brushed in a long time.

B.J. was glad that he hadn't ordered food because he would've lost his appetite. "All right then."

B.J. stood as Woody continued to smile while looking up at him. Woody had enough food for three people set on the table before him, and the bill was already paid.

"Enjoy your meal. I'll be in touch later this week."

"Wonderful. I can't wait to hear from you."

Something in B.J. didn't feel quite right as he turned to exit the diner. There was a queasiness that almost made him change his mind and cancel their agreement. He'd met other gamers online who might be equally as qualified as Woody to assist with his project. But—and this was a big but—they would probably cost him a lot more money, money that he didn't have. So B.J. swallowed his doubts and drove back to Oklahoma, choosing to think about his possible wealth throughout the trip. It was a choice he made in direct opposition to his nagging suspicions. And he had no one else to blame for his stupidity when Woody took his money and then went ghost on him.

Chapter 4

After the Sheriff left, Fern went into the kitchen to check on the spaghetti. As she stirred the simmering food, she continued to worry about the condoms and their implications. She'd said that she would take Pat's advice, but she truly hadn't made up her mind. The fact that Cricket, who was usually so sensible, had condoms and might even be…Lord, she couldn't even bring herself to finish the thought. She needed more time to think about how or whether to address the matter. Gone were the days when a hard swat on the butt or grounding would resolve the issue. Things had gotten much more complicated now that she was dealing with a teenager.

Her stirring motion began to slow down as a different line of thought emerged. Maybe she was being overly sensitive, but it almost seemed like Pat had been treating her like a suspect. He hadn't accused her of any wrongdoing, but something about the way he had watched her had given her the heebie-jeebies. She knew that she shouldn't let it bother her, though. She had nothing to hide. Her hands were as clean as newly minted pennies. And he was welcome to turn over any and every rock he wanted to while searching for Woody and Cricket's car.

The bigger question was whether Woody's hands were clean. What in the world were those pills in the shoebox? Had he turned into a dope fiend behind closed doors? Was he selling drugs? The truth was that she didn't know much about him these days. And she had been fine with that—until the Sheriff had found the pills. Now she needed to know what was going on with Woody, especially if his activities could lead criminals to her home.

She turned off the stove burner and reached for the phone with a mind to call Calvin, but it began to ring before she got a hand on it. She glanced at the caller ID screen and saw that it was her sister, Jasmine. "Hello."

"Hey, girl. I just heard that Woody is missing."

"Really? Who told you?" Yet again, Fern was reminded that there were no secrets in a small town.

"Daddy did. Why haven't you called us?"

"Because I don't think that he's missing. I think that he's laying up somewhere and doesn't give a flip that his family is worried about him. And the worst part is that he has Cricket's car."

"That's what Daddy said. He took off in Cricket's car."

"How does Daddy know that?"

"He said that Turnip told him, and Turnip heard about it from Big Earl."

"Well, how did Big Earl hear about it?"

"Probably from Bonnie. You know she got a job at the police station last year." Bonnie was Big Earl's daughter and, lately, the town's bigmouth crier. "Daddy said that Woody is probably pushing up daisies now."

"I doubt that very seriously. And I don't see how Daddy could think such a thing." Under the circumstances, her father's comment was more than troublesome.

"Because he says that a lot of people around town are mad at Woody. He's been borrowing money, and he never pays them back."

This was the first that Fern had heard about Woody getting money from anyone except his mother. And she wasn't quick to believe it. "I don't think that's true, Jaz. I would've heard about it from somebody."

"Not necessarily. People might be keeping stuff from you because they don't want to upset you."

"So you'd heard about him borrowing money?"

"No. If they don't want you to know, they're not going to tell me."

Fern huffed melodramatically. "Nobody with marbles would loan money to Woody. He hasn't worked in three years. How could he possibly pay them back?"

"I have no clue. I'm just telling you what Daddy said."

At this point, Fern had to wonder if Daddy was intentionally misdirecting people to hide something he'd done. She prayed that she was wrong, but he could be as sly as a fox when he wanted to be.

"Anyway, I know how much you rely on Cricket to help out with Thad and Hope. And since her car is gone, I thought y'all might like to use my old Chevy."

"That would be a big load off my shoulders. Jaz, you're a lifesaver."

"It's all good. I'll bring it by this afternoon when Cricket gets home from school. Tell her to call me."

"Thank you." Fern already felt lighter. "I appreciate this so much. More than you could ever know."

"I do know. I don't have to walk in your shoes to understand what Woody is putting you through. We'd all like to string him up."

"I know, I know." Fern just hoped that no one had acted on their worst impulses.

"I'll talk to you later. I've gotta get some work done." Unlike Fern, Jasmine had a typical nine-to-five job as a paralegal. Not only was she good at it, but her income was at least four times greater than Fern's.

"All right. Thanks again." Fern hung up the phone and rolled her shoulders in an attempt to relax them. She hadn't realized how tense she was until Jasmine offered her spare car. Now that Cricket would be able to resume taking Hope and Thad to their sporting practices and games, a huge stressor had been removed. And Fern suddenly felt more worn out than she had been in years. She placed a note on the refrigerator for Cricket to call Jasmine and then went to bed. Assuming that Woody didn't show up before she left for work, she would call Calvin later.

"I'm telling you, Sheriff, I don't know where he is." Calvin, a lanky, ruddy man, was tall enough to be a pro basketball player. As such, he towered over Pat, who knew he wasn't getting the whole truth. Although Calvin maintained eye contact throughout their conversation, he kept blinking in flurries after answering Pat's questions.

"So you took him to the stadium to get Cricket's car. And he never once told you where he was going when he got it. I find that extremely hard to believe since you two grew up together."

"But it's the truth." Calvin wiped his greasy hands on a towel. As a mechanic, he was currently covered in filth since Pat had come to his job to question him about Woody.

"Has he been experimenting with any drugs lately? Could he be a danger to himself?"

"No, sir. Woody likes his bourbon and beer. That's why he's got that beachball bulge."

"But no drugs whatsoever?"

"Just pot."

Pat shook his head and walked to the garage opening for fresh air. He had been here for over an hour patiently prodding Calvin and had gotten nowhere. If Calvin knew anything, he wasn't going to squeal. Pat decided to try a different tactic, one designed to pull his heartstrings. He turned back around and saw that Calvin was now leaning over a car, and tinkering with tubes under the hood. "You know, his wife is mighty worried about him. She sure would like to know if he's coming home."

Calvin immediately laughed without lifting his head from his task. "Fern couldn't care less where Woody is. I care more than she does."

"Is that something Woody told you?"

"That's something Woody and everyone in town knows. Including you." He stood straight again and picked up the towel. "I just remembered something, though. When I saw Woody on Friday night, he said that he and Fern had had a big knock-down-drag-out about him taking Cricket's car. And she said something like she would kill him if he took it."

"Oh?" Fern had not mentioned any of this to Pat when they had spoken earlier.

"Yeah! She sure did. Woody and I just laughed about it. Those two argue all the time, so we didn't take her seriously. But now...I don't know. Maybe she did do something to him. Maybe he's not missing." Calvin frowned as the first signs of genuine concern creased his brow. "Maybe he's dead."

Although Pat flirted with the same suspicion, he wasn't going to reveal that to Calvin. "Or maybe he decided he'd had enough and cut out."

"No way. Woody wouldn't give up that free meal ticket. I've tried to talk him into leaving several times. I even offered him a job here, but he's set in his ways. You know what I'm saying? Can't tell him nothing."

"Has anyone else ever threatened him? Or gotten upset enough to want to hurt him?"

"Almost everyone in Fern's family. People have been gossiping about it for years. I'm sure you heard that her father wants to shoot him."

Pat had forgotten about that, but he did vaguely remember that Deputy Perkins had been called to the house after Woody struck Fern. He'd spent one night in jail before Fern had dropped all the charges, but that didn't mean all was forgiven. As a father of three daughters himself, he knew that any men dumb enough to bang them up wouldn't be alive to talk about it. He also knew without a shadow of doubt that Fern's father, Hiram, felt the same way. "I do recall hearing that, but I thought he had cooled off by now."

"Not according to Woody. Every time they see each other, Woody says that Mr. Bennett gives him the eye. So Woody won't go to his house anymore. And he sure as hell doesn't want to be alone with him."

"I see." The case was getting more complicated by the minute. "Has Woody been seeing any women other than Fern?"

"Only the kind you pay for, Sheriff. The kind that keep their legs open and their mouths closed." He returned his attention to the car.

"Where'd he get the money for that?"

"From his mama—without her knowledge. And I admit, I've given him a few bucks, too. So has Roy. A man's gotta do what a man's gotta do when he ain't getting no nooky at home." He shot a knowing look at Pat. "We're still in our prime. You feel me?"

Pat understood, but those days were long behind him. "Give me the names of the women he's been sleeping with. I need to speak with them."

"I've never asked for their names. And even if I did know 'em, I wouldn't tell you."

"But your cooperation could make the difference between life and death for your friend. Don't you want to help me find him?"

"Woody doesn't pay those women to talk. And if he's dead, we both know that it wouldn't be at the hands of a prostitute."

His efforts confounded, Pat was forced to part ways with Calvin empty-handed. Regardless of the good he might've done his friend by being forthright with Pat, his lips were zipped. But his obstinance wouldn't stop Pat from learning more about the pills that he'd secured from Woody's house. At this very moment, they were on their way to a lab in Houston where their composition would be analyzed. While he waited for the results, Pat would continue to do his job and question anyone who might put him on Woody's trail. Despite sharing Calvin's misgivings about Fern and her family, he couldn't rule out the possibility that Woody had gotten in over his head with some sort of racket and skipped town.

After eating a sauerkraut sandwich in his car, he headed back to Woody's home to speak with Cricket. Since she was just a kid, he would take it easy on her. He rang the doorbell and smiled when she answered the door, wanting to show a friendly face that might assuage her concerns. "Hello, Cricket. Did Fern tell you that I was coming by to talk to you today?"

She didn't return his smile. "No, sir. Did you find my dad yet?"

"Unfortunately, no. I was hoping that we could talk about the last time you saw him. It might help me a great deal."

"Okay." Rather than invite him in, she stepped outside onto the porch. Unlike Fern, she seemed to be extremely upset. She pushed her shoulder-length hair behind her ears and crossed her arms.

"Your mother told me that you saw Woody Friday night when he came for your car at the high school football game. Is that right?"

"Yes, sir. He took my car, and we haven't seen him since." Her lip quivered, and she swiped her nose.

She could break down at any moment, and Pat knew he must tread lightly. "How did he seem to be feeling when you saw him?"

"He seemed okay, maybe a little nervous."

"Do you know why he might've been nervous?"

"No, sir. He doesn't talk much when he's here."

"But you had the clear impression that he was nervous?"

"Yes, sir."

Pat could infer a few different reasons why Woody would be nervous, the most obvious being the pills in the shoebox. He again wondered if Woody, dimwit that he was, had bitten off more than he could chew. As long as the car wasn't found, there was a good chance that Woody was alive and on the run.

Of course, there was an equal chance that he was buried in the woods somewhere.

"Did he happen to say anything about where he was going?"

"No, sir. But my best friend, Cindy, said her father's barber heard that a UFO abducted him."

"Who heard that? Her father?"

"The barber, Mr. Burns. He says that Mr. Wright's wife saw bright lights in the sky on the night Daddy went missing. And they think that some aliens got him." Now she wiped both eyes as tears began to fall. "Do you think it's true, Sheriff?"

"Of course not. That's not true at all. People are just trying to figure out where your dad is. And sometimes they start imagining things that didn't happen." He placed his hands on his knees and leaned down to face her at eye level. "I promise you that I'm going to find Woody. And I fully expect him to be perfectly fine when I do. So don't you worry, okay?"

"Okay." She sniffled and wiped her eyes again. "I was mad at him for taking my car, but I'm not mad now. I just want him to come home."

"I know that. And I'm sure that he does, too." He stood upright once again. "How often does he use your car?"

"Not much. Sometimes he uses it to go buy a pack of beer since Mama won't buy it for him. But he always comes right back. At least, I think he does."

"You're not sure?"

"No, sir. If he left and came back after I went to bed, I wouldn't know."

"Do you have any reason to think he uses the car while you're asleep?"

She nodded hesitantly. "I keep the gas tank at least half-full because I don't ever want to run out. And there's been times when the tank was a quarter full when I drove to school. I could've forgotten to pay attention, though." Everything about her body language suggested that she didn't forget.

"Do you remember what he was wearing when you saw him?"

"I think he had on jeans and a black jacket. That's what he wears most of the time."

"And what time did he leave?"

"Around eight o'clock."

"Was he alone?"

"He came with Mr. Woods, and then Mama came right after they left."

"Oh?" Another tidbit that Fern had neglected to share when they had spoken earlier. "She didn't work on Friday night?"

"She went to work and then left because Daddy took my car. She wanted to make sure I had a ride home."

This information seemed to corroborate Calvin's statement that Fern and Woody had argued about the car. She must've been piping mad that Cricket would be stranded. "Did Fern know why Woody needed the car?"

"I don't know."

Before Pat could ask his last question, a blue Chevy sedan pulled into the driveway, drawing his and Cricket's attention. He immediately recognized the driver as Fern's sister, Jasmine, who was quite the whippersnapper. To the best of his knowledge, she was still single, and as sharp as a tack—which was probably why she was still single. There weren't too many men in town who could endure her uppity spirit.

"Hello there, Sheriff. I didn't expect to see you." Jasmine sauntered over to them without taking her eyes off of Pat. She was a good-looking woman with an hourglass figure. But woe unto the man who made the mistake of thinking that her beauty wasn't matched by her brain.

"Hello, Jasmine. I'm sorry to say that I'm here to investigate Woody's disappearance."

"Well, obviously you won't find him here." She stepped onto the porch and draped a protective arm around Cricket. "Shouldn't you be talking to people at bars and GameStop? You'd get further a lot faster than picking a child's mind."

"I'll get around to that." Pat didn't want to have a testy exchange with Jasmine in front of Cricket, who was clearly fragile. He decided to conclude his questions of Cricket and take advantage of Jasmine's unexpected arrival. "Since you're here, would you tell me when you last saw Woody?"

"I don't remember. He stopped coming around the family months ago."

"And why was that?"

"I don't know. You'd have to ask Woody."

He needn't prod this particular question since Calvin had already told him why. Jasmine had merely confirmed another detail in Calvin's statement. "You don't come here to see Fern and the kids?"

"Not very often. I don't like being around a slimeball who slapped my sister."

"So with the exception of Fern and their kids, no one in your family has seen him for the last—I don't know—six or seven months?"

"Not that I know of."

"That's pretty hard to believe since the town is no bigger than a bull's butt. Even if Woody went out of his way to avoid every single one of you, somebody would've bumped into him somewhere at some point."

"That may be true. But if they did see him, I didn't hear about it."

Jasmine came off as defensive, which didn't make any sense—unless she was hiding something. Maybe she knew exactly where Woody was. And maybe she knew because either she or someone in her family had bumped him off.

Pat looked from Jasmine to Cricket, who was hanging her head as low as it could go without falling off. Were she not present, he would try to tease an incriminating comment out of her aunt. But it could wait. Jasmine wasn't going anywhere, and he had plenty of people to interview. He would shuffle the order around, though. Instead of speaking with Roy next as he had planned, he was going to pay a visit to Bernie's Bistro. Now that he knew Fern had spoken to Woody and then left her job on Friday night, he wanted to know what her coworkers may have heard or seen.

Chapter 5

Having contended with bloodsucking freeloaders in his family, B.J. should've heeded the signs that Woody was one and the same. His eagerness to provide gaming expertise for merely two grand and no other stakes had been too good to be true. Now B.J. was out one grand with nothing to show for it—but Woody would not be getting off scot-free as he seemed to expect. Just as B.J. has misjudged Woody, it was obvious that Woody had misjudged him. And there would be hell to pay if Woody didn't return every cent of B.J.'s money.

Upon realizing that Woody had deliberately stopped responding to his chatroom messages, B.J. had used his network of contacts to obtain Woody's home address and unlisted phone number. He'd then called the house several times, but had been consistently informed that Woody wasn't home. It was an unfortunate series of events that would not end well for Woody. He had double-crossed the wrong man. Before loading his rifle and a change of clothes into his truck, B.J. had given Woody one last chance to answer a chatroom message, the tone of which had fallen just short of threatening murder. But yet again, B.J.'s effort had been futile. So he'd hit the road, seeing red all the way from Oklahoma to the front door of Woody's house. Finding no signs of life after ringing the doorbell, he went back to his truck and parked a little way up the street, where he was near enough to see without being seen. From there, he would wait and watch for Woody. As a proficient hunter, he was good at waiting and he was good at watching for his prey.

Her shift at work had been busier than usual, affording Fern no time to call Calvin. She was sure that he knew what Woody was up to, but she wasn't keen on talking to him again. When they'd spoken yesterday, she could feel his hatred for her through the phone line, and only a loon would voluntarily subject themselves to such despisal. But she was beginning to feel a desperation that gave her no choice but to set aside her reservations and call him when she got back home.

As the phone rang, she subconsciously breathed heavier, dreading another conversation with him. Like Woody, she had known Calvin since childhood, but they had never gotten along. Fern had been the proverbial good girl, and Calvin had earned a reputation as a hoodlum who'd regularly skipped school. According to rumors, he had sold drugs but had gone clean after serving a couple of stints in juvenile detention. Nowadays he was generally regarded as an honest citizen, which might only mean that he had gotten better at hiding his illicit activities. And since Woody was a follower, he was prone to do whatever Calvin was doing—especially if he could make some easy money at it.

"Woody! Man, I'm glad you called." On answering the phone, Calvin dispensed with all customary salutations, apparently reacting to the number that had appeared on his caller ID. "Everybody's been worried about you!"

"It's not Woody. It's Fern."

"Fern?" Disgust immediately permeated his voice. "What the hell are you calling me for again?"

"I need to talk to you about Woody."

"He's still not back home?"

"If he were here, I wouldn't be calling you." She heard him grunt with frustration.

"What have you done to him, Fern? And don't lie. The whole town knows that you've done something. Is he dead?"

"I have no idea! And no one should think that I've done anything because it couldn't be further from the truth!" She was downright appalled at the accusation.

"Oh yeah? Patsy came by my shop today and said that she'd heard about your threat to stab him. She said that you told him that he better not go to sleep. I guess you actually did it, didn't you?"

"Of course not! I would never do such a thing! And I've never threatened to stab him." Fern was so taken aback that she forgot why she had called Calvin. "I would never harm the father of my children! If anything, I was the one in danger, seeing as how he had started hitting me."

"He only hit you one time. And I told him then that he needed to leave. We both knew that he might get killed after that. You were just biding your time, letting the dust settle so no one would finger you. I know it, and so does the Sheriff."

"How could anybody know about something that didn't happen? That's ridiculous!"

"He knows it because I told him. Don't play dumb, Fern. Either you or some crazy clown in your family took Woody out. And I'll bet you've made damn sure that his body will never be found."

"You actually told the Sheriff that we killed Woody?" By now, Fern's breathing had become so labored that she had to sit down.

"That's right. And pretty soon, he's going to crawl up your ass to find the truth. So you better get ready!" Calvin slammed the phone down before Fern could say anything else.

She couldn't believe what Calvin had just told her. Not only had she been accused of murdering Woody, but the Sheriff might believe him. Her freedom could be in jeopardy. Her kids could be forced to grow up without her. For several minutes, she felt woozy and remained frozen at the kitchen table until Thad lumbered in looking for breakfast.

"Hey, Mama."

"Good morning, sweetheart." Fern jumped up and rushed toward her bedroom to make a private phone call.

"You're not making breakfast this morning?"

"No. Get yourself some cereal. There's plenty in the pantry."

She closed her bedroom door behind her and called the Sheriff's office. "Hi, Dottie. Is the Sheriff in yet?"

"No, he won't be here until around ten thirty. Do you want to leave a message for him to call you?"

"It's sort of urgent that I speak to him. Can I get his cell phone number please?"

"Sure." Dottie gave Fern the number.

"Thanks, Dottie." Fern wasted no time calling him, but was routed to his voicemail. Frantic, she left a message for him to call her back as soon as possible. It seemed that her heebie-jeebies yesterday had been an ominous premonition.

Pat had just stepped into Bernie's Bistro when his cell phone started to vibrate with an incoming call. When he saw that it originated from the Walker house, he knew that he wasn't answering it. He nonchalantly placed it back in his pocket as Jared rushed toward him.

"Mornin', Sheriff."

"Good morning, Jared. Can I get a booth please?"

"Absolutely. Will you be dining alone? Or is someone joining you?"

"It's just me."

"All right. Follow me."

Jared led him to one of the smaller booths that offered a view of the parking lot. After taking Pat's order for coffee, he sped away as Pat took in his surroundings. The place was buzzing with a decent number of customers, most of them truckers, it seemed. Bernie had smartly chosen this location precisely because it was near an interstate highway that ran straight to Mexico. And when the foot traffic got heavy near the border, this was a convenient place for Pat to surveil it.

Jared returned with a coffee mug and began filling it. "Are you ready to order, or do you need a few minutes to look at the menu?"

"I'm not here to eat, Jared. I'm here to ask you and your coworkers some questions."

"Oh? What about?"

"Woody Walker. I'm sure you've heard that he's missing."

"I know that he stole Cricket's car."

"Well, that, too. But more importantly, a human being is missing."

"Woody is more of a creature from the Black Lagoon than a human being, Sheriff. Tony and I both think that Fern is better off without him." Tony was Jared's longtime boyfriend. "Goodbye and good riddance is what we say."

"That may well be true, but I still need to find out where he is. And if you know anything that might help my investigation, then you need to tell me." Pat drank from the mug while watching Jared closely. He knew that the waitstaff here were chummy. And they may not be inclined to divulge any secrets that Fern had shared. But he would know if they were lying to him. There were always dead giveaways. He only needed to pay attention.

"I'm sorry, Sheriff, but I don't know a thing."

Pat paused. "I heard that you were here the other night when Woody called to speak with Fern."

"Yeah, I was. So?"

"So, what happened that night?"

"There's not much to tell." Jared shifted his weight from one foot to the other and broke eye contact—clear signs to Pat that whatever came out of his mouth was going to be either evasive or an outright lie. "He called to speak with Fern, and they spoke."

"How did Fern react to their conversation?"

"Oh, I don't know. She may have been a little upset, but that's nothing new. Woody always upsets Fern."

"Upset enough to leave the diner?"

"No, she's used to his antics. She vents for a little while, but then she gets over it."

"But she did leave on that night, didn't she?"

Jared drew his lips into a line as he thought about the question. "You know what? You're right. She did leave that night. It must've slipped my mind."

"I'm sure it did." Pat's disbelief was obvious. "What did she leave to do?"

"She didn't say."

"What kind of mood was she in when she left?"

"Uh—" He again appeared to search his memory. "I honestly just don't remember, Sheriff. I work so much that the days practically run together. In fact, I can barely remember what I ate for dinner last night."

"Okay, then who else was working that night?"

Jared's face scrunched up. "To tell you the truth—"

"You don't remember."

"No, sorry."

"Is Bernie here?" Pat was finished with Jared's selective memory. He knew that Bernie respected the law and would share any and all information available. And it was best that some of Pat's requests be made directly to the business owner anyway.

"Not at the moment. He's scheduled to come in at noon today."

"All right. I'll come back around then." He reached for his wallet to pay for the coffee.

"No, no, Sheriff. The coffee is on us."

He stood up and restored the wallet to his pocket. "Thank you."

"Of course. We appreciate your service to the community."

Pat gave Jared a dubious look and then left without another word.

Beset with nervous energy, Fern busied herself with tidying up her home while she waited for the Sheriff to return her call. Admittedly, there wasn't much to do without Woody around making messes, which normally would've been a good thing. But this was one time she wouldn't mind having more messes to clean. To avoid going stir-crazy, she put her back into scrubbing the baseboards better than she ever had before. She had worked up a good sweat when the doorbell rang, giving her a moment's hope that Pat had decided to stop by in person.

When she opened the door and saw a bedraggled stranger standing there, her disappointment couldn't've been greater. His scraggly appearance instantly put her on alert. "Can I help you?"

"Hello there, ma'am. My name is B.J., and I'm looking for Woody. Is he at home?"

"No, not at the moment."

"Aw, that's too bad. Can you tell me when he'll be back?"

"I don't have an exact time, but he could be back at any minute. Is he expecting you?" Fern wondered if he had come in search of drugs, a bone-chilling thought that caused her knees to knock. She slowly brought the door closer to her body, attempting to shield the inside of her house from his view. Given his height, though, it was a wasted effort. He looked like a walking, talking bulldozer.

"No, ma'am, he's not. I'm in town for a couple of days and thought I'd look him up while I'm here."

"I know all of Woody's friends, and he's never mentioned you. Why do you want to see him?" As his wife, she was entitled to know why B.J. had come to her home, but she was torn between needing to know and badly wanting him off of her property.

"Well, we have some business to settle, just between us." He looked over her head and into the house, causing her to reflexively bring the door even closer to her body, further narrowing his view.

"What kind of business?"

He again looked at her and sort of smiled without actually smiling. "I'll come back later. Can I ask you to do me a favor? Fern, right? Your name is Fern?"

"Yes, that's right."

"It's a pleasure to meet you, Fern. If you see Woody before I do, would you please tell him that B.J. is looking for him and that I'll be back so we can talk?"

Something told Fern that Woody wouldn't want to be anywhere within a hundred miles of B.J. "S-sure," she stammered, sensing menace despite his polite language.

He touched the tip of his baseball cap in a wordless farewell and then turned to walk toward the street. By now, Fern was a nervous wreck and couldn't close her door fast enough. Relieved that he had left without any trouble, she knew that her first impression about B.J. had been wrong—he was not a drug addict. He was something worse, something deadly. She didn't know what Woody had done to piss him off, but he might be the reason that Woody had hit the hills. She would be sure to tell Pat about him as soon as he called.

Just then, the phone rang and scared the living daylights out of Fern. She quickly gathered herself and raced to answer it, hoping that it was Pat. "Hello?"

"Hello yourself. How's it going?"

It was Jared. "Dadgummit! I was hoping you'd be the Sheriff. I really need to speak with him."

"Why? Something happen?"

"Yeah, maybe. I'm not sure. Some big, weird guy just came here looking for Woody, and I think Pat should talk to him."

"I wish that I knew where Woody was so I could point that guy in the right direction."

"This isn't the time for jokes, Jared. I spoke with Calvin earlier this morning, and he claims to have told the Sheriff that I probably killed Woody. Can you believe that?"

"Oh... That explains why the Sheriff was asking a lot of questions about you this morning. I was calling to warn you."

"Oh, God." Fern suddenly felt limp. "What kind of questions?"

"He wanted to know why you left work the night that Woody disappeared. And if you were upset when you left."

"What did you tell him?"

"I told him I don't remember anything."

"Why'd you do that?" Fern's fears began to intensify. "You should've told him whatever he wanted to know. Otherwise, he'll think I'm guilty of something."

"Okay, well—I thought that I was helping you."

"No, you're not helping me! I haven't done anything! I don't know where Woody is, and that's the truth."

"I don't think the Sheriff believes that, Fern. So we're going to have to circle our wagons to make sure he doesn't arrest you."

"Are you saying that I need to lie so that he doesn't find out that I didn't kill Woody?"

"No, you keep telling him that. But I'm not going to tell him how mad you were when you left the restaurant that night. And I'm definitely not going to tell him that you said you would kill him. Somebody else must've told him, though. Maybe one of the customers."

"People get mad and threaten to kill each other all the time! It's an idle threat." Her fear was beginning to morph into anger. "There weren't many people at the diner when I left. Who could've told the Sheriff that I threatened Woody?"

"Let's see...Lionel was here, Joanie, Satchel, Francisco—"

"Forget I asked. It doesn't matter because I didn't do anything to Woody. And while everyone is accusing me, that man is riding around God knows where in Cricket's car, a car that was not his to take. And this fact seems to have gotten lost."

"The Sheriff thinks that Woody matters more than the car."

"That's because he's not married to him."

"Amen to that."

Jared's loyal commiseration did nothing to stop her emotions from flying everywhere at once. Fern used her free hand to cover her eyes. This whole thing was turning into a turdball that was rolling downhill fast and getting bigger by the minute. If she didn't stop it soon, her life, her livelihood, her children's future, everything could be in jeopardy. She glumly thanked Jared for standing guard before they exchanged goodbyes. Then she placed more futile calls to both the police station and the Sheriff's cell phone, more determined than ever to speak with the man who might hold her fate in his hands.

The second time Fern called his cell phone, Pat was in the process of parking in Roy's driveway—or more correctly, his parents' driveway. As with his pal Woody, Roy didn't have a job. Despite closing in on age forty, he still lived with his parents, Maggie and Roy Sr., in their large, eight-bedroom home. They all seemed to be as snug as a bug in a rug, as Pat had never heard any complaints about Roy being a leech. His easy living had probably inspired Woody to attempt the same. Too bad for Woody that his financial circumstances simply did not enable him to kick back like a prince. And Fern had left no doubt among any of the town's residents that Woody was dead weight—maybe literally now.

Pat rang the doorbell and looked around while waiting for someone to open the door. He knew that everyone was home, but soon Roy Sr. would be leaving to play a round of golf while

Maggie gardened in the front yard. He didn't really know what Roy Jr. did all day.

Maggie answered the door with her gardening hat in her hands and obvious surprise at finding Pat on her doorstep. Her skin was nearly as pale as an eggshell, and Pat marveled that she withstood the sun without burning to a crisp.

"Good morning, Sheriff. How can I help you?"

"Mornin', Maggie. I'm investigating the disappearance of Woody Walker, and I need to speak with your son. Is he around?"

"Sure, sure." She stepped aside so that Pat could enter the spacious foyer. "R.J. is outside by the pool." She began walking toward the back of the house as Pat followed. "It's just terrible that Woody is missing. R.J. has been worried sick for days. Are you close to finding him?"

"I'm running down every lead, and I have every reason to believe that Woody will be found safe."

"Oh, really? That's interesting because I heard that he had died of alcohol poisoning. He was known to hit the bottle pretty hard while poor Fern worked her fingers to the bone."

"Who said he was dead?"

"Sheriff, everyone thinks that he's dead. Don't you?" They reached a sliding glass door, and stepped outside without Maggie waiting for Pat's response. Roy was sitting on a lounge chair next to the pool, drinking a margarita for breakfast. "R.J., honey, the Sheriff is here to talk to you about Woody."

Roy turned his head to see his visitor. "Oh yeah? Well, have a seat, Sheriff." He pointed to a lounge chair near him. "Can we get you anything to drink? You wanna have what I'm having?"

"No, I don't touch the stuff while I'm working." Pat sat down and sized Roy up. He was as skinny as a rail, his light-brown hair was perpetually uncombed, and his lips were as red as cherries. To Pat, he was strange-looking, but most of the women thought he was boyishly handsome. At least, that's what they said. But they were more likely attracted to his guaranteed inheritance. His family was one of very few in Luna with enough money to buy the town if they wanted to. And everything had always been handed to Roy on a silver platter. Pat fully expected Roy to indulge in every bite on that platter until he died from gluttony.

"Would you like something else, Sheriff? I've still got some hot coffee in the kitchen."

"No, thank you, Maggie. I won't be here long."

"All right then." She went back inside, most likely on her way to the flowerbeds in the front.

"Roy, I know how close you and Woody are. And I know you're worried about him. I'm here for your help to find him. Do you know anything that might help my investigation?"

"I know the same thing that everyone else knows." He seemed to be a little tipsy, which might loosen up his tongue if Pat was lucky. "Either Fern's wacky daddy or her psycho sister has shot him. Woody's gone, Sheriff. He's gone, and he ain't coming back. You of all people know it."

"What makes you think that Fern's family has killed him?"

"Because they've been threatening to kill him for a year! And they don't play with a full deck, you know what I'm saying? They're sociopaths, and Woody was number one on their hit list."

"Why would that be?"

"Because they don't like him. They've never liked him. He's too good for that bunch, Sheriff. And that Jasmine—" He dramatically slapped the chair's arm. "That one acts like she's so smart. She's been trying to turn Fern against Woody for a long time, but it never works. You know why? Because Woody knows how to keep Fern in her place. The good book says that a wife must forsake all others for her husband. And Fern has to obey him whether or not her family likes him. That's the way it is."

Pat could see that Roy had a distorted view of reality, and he now worried that a conversation with him might actually be a conversation with the bottle. "So you think that Jasmine killed Woody because Woody is smarter than she is?"

"I'll tell you what I think, Sheriff. I think that Jasmine and her daddy cooked up a plan to put him down like a sick horse. They put a bullet square in the middle of his forehead and left him somewhere for the animals to pick his bones dry. That's what I think. You need to be looking into them because they've got blood on their hands. I'm sure of it."

"Did Woody ever tell you that he was in fear for his life?"

"All the time! Hell, there were some nights that he was scared to go to sleep at his own house. He thought that someone was going to sneak in and drag him off while Fern was at work with an airtight alibi."

Pat exhaled long and hard. "Roy, I want you to shoot it straight with me. Was Woody into anything dangerous?"

"Like what?"

"I don't know. Maybe drugs?"

"Woody?" Roy looked genuinely stunned at the suggestion. "No way, man. Not Woody." He chugged the margarita and dragged the back of his arm over his mouth. It was a nervous reaction that told Pat that he was lying through his teeth. As with Calvin, it seemed that Roy's helpfulness had its limits. Nobody was going to fess up to having knowledge of something that could suck them into the mud.

"I understand from Calvin that Woody had relationships with women other than Fern. What do you know about that?"

Roy snickered. "Fern wouldn't let him touch her, but he still got his fair share of trim. Yes, sir, he sure did."

"Do you know who he was seeing?"

"The only woman he ever mentioned to me was Shasta Monet. She moved to town a couple of years ago and took real good care of him." He snickered again.

Pat knew about her. She kept a low profile, but her services were no secret to any of the town's men. "When was the last time you spoke to Woody?"

"The day before he went missing. I should've gone by to check on him because I could tell that something wasn't right. He seemed like he was scared, but he didn't tell me what was going on. I just figured that Fern's family was at it again, calling the house and making threats."

"They've been calling him?"

"They call when Fern goes to work. They pretend like they're calling to speak to the kids, but if Woody answers the phone, all hell breaks loose."

"How long has this been going on?"

"For a while now, Sheriff. I'm telling you they hate him. And they've been waiting for a chance to get away with murder so they can spit on his grave."

Chapter 6

Lips were flapping all over town, and Pat would swear that they had generated a headwind. Although he was accustomed to ignoring local mania, the increasingly morbid speculations about Woody added fuel to his growing sense of urgency. On the strength of Roy's divulgence, he decided to drop by Shasta's place, hoping to find Woody there enjoying a prolonged spree of sorts. While he would never reveal such unrefined behavior to Fern, at least he could tell her and Liddie that Woody was alive and well—not that Fern would care. And since he'd thought about arresting Shasta more than a few times, he knew exactly where she lived.

He called Dottie to alert her to his plans, at which point she told him about Fern's repeated calls. As Fern was now a prime person of interest in his investigation, he wasn't yet ready to speak with her again. The conversation would likely turn into an interrogation, and he needed to have his ducks in a row.

Pat arrived at Shasta's apartment complex, and stretched his back before walking up a flight of stairs to her front door.

In keeping with her low profile, she lived in a moderately expensive area where almost everything one needed was within walking distance. She had no vehicle that he was aware of nor had she bothered to make any friends. Whatever she had left behind in Louisiana must've taught her a lesson about getting too close to anyone.

He knocked on her door and heard a small dog begin to yap from inside the apartment. After a short wait, she opened the door wearing daisy dukes and a T-shirt with "Finger lickin' good" on it. The last time he'd seen her, she'd worn her black hair in braids that trailed down her back. Now her hair was purple and pulled up into a braided bun. Ordinarily, Pat wouldn't have liked the look, but on Shasta, everything looked good.

"Howdy, Sheriff. To what do I owe the pleasure of your visit?" She licked a lollipop suggestively, and his mouth almost went dry.

"I'm trying to locate Woody Walker. He's been missing for four days, and I heard that you've been seeing him."

"I haven't seen Woody in weeks." She picked up her dog, a white toy poodle. "Do you wanna come in?"

"No, thank you." Actually, he would've liked to look around her apartment, but he knew that he would never live down the rumors if anyone saw him exit Shasta's apartment alone.

Anyway, the fact that she had invited him in suggested that she was on the up and up, so there was probably nothing to see.

"Suit yourself." She continued to enthusiastically enjoy her lollipop, and Pat's eyes were riveted to her mouth longer than he realized. "Do you need to know anything else?"

"Yes, I do." He cleared this throat and compelled himself to hold fast to his sense of decency. "When you last saw Woody, did he say anything to you about leaving town?"

"Of course not. Woody has never lived anywhere but Luna, and he's going to die in Luna."

"Did he ever mention his wife to you?"

"Only to say that he wishes he'd never gotten married. I don't think she's very interested in pleasing him."

"Obviously."

"He was scared out of his mind of her father, though. I can't even count the number of times he came over here just to sleep at night."

"Really?"

"Uh-huh. I felt sorry for him, so I let him stay—as long as I wasn't busy."

"I see. So he thought that his life was in danger?"

"That's what he said. Her whole family was out to get him."

"And what about his wife? Was he concerned about her trying to harm him?"

"Sheriff, he thinks that they all want him dead. But Fern would never have the guts to pull the trigger if it came down to that. She might poison him, though. I could see her doing something like that."

Pat's blood ran cold at the notion. "Did Woody think that she was poisoning him?"

"No, I just said that I could see her doing that because that's the way women operate. And growing up in Baton Rouge, I heard about all kinds of shady ways to kill people—voodoo, hit men, drowning, car accidents, you name it. But women almost always prefer poison, especially if they're doing the killing."

"Did Woody ever show signs of being poisoned?"

"I wouldn't know, Sheriff, since I've never poisoned anyone."

Pat nodded while ruminating on her statements.

"If I hear from Woody, I'll tell him to get in touch with you." She peered behind him as if she was expecting someone. Pat was almost certain that his presence was hindering a john from keeping an appointment.

"That would be much obliged." He started to leave but paused. "Shasta, have you ever thought about getting a real job?"

"Whatever do you mean?" She batted her long, fake eyelashes and smiled at him without losing a grip on the lollipop.

"I mean a job that pays taxable wages. A job that you could tell your mother about."

"My mother doesn't care what I do as long as I don't ask her for anything."

"Well, I'm sure that your father wouldn't be happy to know how his little girl is making a living. You ever think about that?"

"All I think about is me. Everything else is irrelevant."

He stepped a little closer to her. "The only reason I haven't busted you is because you gave me the intel I needed to close a case last year. But my gratitude won't last forever. Consider yourself warned."

She squinted her eyes and bit into the lollipop as he turned away. He had planned to go back to Bernie's Bistro, but now he thought better of it. Instead, he was going to pay a visit to Fern's father, Hiram.

Yet again, Fern had been unable to sleep as she usually would after cleaning the house. Her mind was running wild with visions of false imprisonment. On top of that, B.J. had really spooked her. Before he'd shown up, she'd assumed that Woody was either laid up drunk or having the time of his life somewhere. Now she realized that his lamebrained antics may have finally caught up with him. He might actually be hurt or dead, waiting to be found, waiting to be rescued or for a toe tag. The prospect was hard to swallow. Although she resented the man, she wouldn't wish such an end to their union. Not this way.

Having abandoned all hope of rest before going to work, Fern got into her car and started driving around town in search of any signs of Woody. She drove to the outskirts near the Mexico border. She drove to all three hotels in town. She drove to his favorite bar. She even drove by his mother's house. Unsurprisingly, she found nothing of note, but she kept on driving anyway.

While on the road and scouring everything in sight, she used her cell phone to call her parents' house. If Pat was going to be breathing down her neck, she was going to need their help. Under normal circumstances, she would rather gnaw her own leg off than ask them for anything. But her pride at being self-sufficient was no match for her fear of going to jail, the thought of which nearly made her cry when her mother answered the phone.

"Hey, Mama. It's Fern."

"Fern! Why didn't you tell me that Woody is missing? Why did I have to hear about that from your father?"

"I'm sorry. He's been doing whatever he wants for so long that I didn't think anything of it. But now—I don't know. Four days is a long time for him to be gone, and I'm starting to worry."

"*Starting* to worry? We're talking about the father of your children, and you're only *starting* to worry about him after four days? Your priorities are not in order. I know that he leaves much to be desired, but you have to think about your children. Jasmine tells me that they're falling apart."

"That's not true." Fern was immediately defensive. "I talk to them every day, and they all understand that we have to wait and see what the Sheriff finds out. For all we know, Woody could be gallivanting around Mexico."

"He could also be lying dead in a sewer."

Fern cringed as a gory image of Woody splayed in excrement popped into her mind.

"Regardless of all his faults," Mama continued, "he's never been gone this long. And I believe that something bad must've happened to him. You need to talk to Cricket, Hope, and Thad about their concerns. Let them know that you're doing everything you can to find Woody."

Fern had heard nothing after "dead in a sewer." If Woody wasn't found, she might have nightmares for the rest of her life. "I need to speak to Daddy."

"Are you going to do what I said?"

"Yes, Mama, I am. I promise." Fern had no idea what Mama had told her to do.

"Good. Hold on while I get your father." She heard her mother calling out for him to pick up the phone.

"Hello?"

"Daddy, thank God." She was rattled, and she knew he would hear it in her voice.

"What's wrong, baby?"

"It's Woody. I know you've heard that he's missing. Mama's mad that I didn't tell y'all, and I'm sorry about that. But I have a bigger problem on my hands. I think that Sheriff Dupree is going to arrest me."

"Arrest you for what? You haven't done anything to that twit!"

"I know that, Daddy, but the Sheriff has been asking a lot of questions at my job, and people are starting to think that he's suspicious of me. My stomach is all tied up in knots. I don't know what I'll do if he takes me away from my children."

"Whatever he thinks, it'll never come to that. You can take that to the bank." She could hear the steely resolve for which her father was well-known. "I will never let anything happen to you or to my grandbabies."

"I appreciate that, but what if—I mean, I think—" She stifled a sniffle as she struggled to speak. "I think I'm going to need a lawyer. It's the only way that I can protect myself."

"Then we'll get you a lawyer. Consider it done."

"Thank you, Daddy," Fern gushed with relief. "I'm on the brink of a nervous breakdown over all of this. I have no idea where Woody is, and the longer he's gone, the worse it looks."

"I'm sure that he'll eventually come crawling back like all cockroaches do."

"I just hope he comes back in one piece. A man came by the house—"

"Honey, I'm sorry," he cut her off. "I've gotta go. Your mother says that we have company."

"Who?"

"I don't know yet. Call me back later or tomorrow morning so we can make arrangements for an attorney."

"Okay, Daddy. I love you." Fern had intended to tell him about B.J. and the box of pills, but she would have to wait until their next conversation. For now, she could at least be comforted by the thought that she would soon have legal representation. Already, she was breathing a lot easier.

Having traveled a good distance from Luna, Fern made a U-turn going back toward town. Altogether, she'd driven at least seventy miles that morning, but she may has well have been standing still. Woody had turned into thin air. Distracted with thoughts of saving her own skin, Fern was paying little attention to her surroundings when a glimmer of something green caught her eye. She turned to get a look at the source and saw an abandoned Coors warehouse. And then she saw something else. She couldn't believe her eyes—it was Cricket's car.

Aghast, Fern made a beeline to the warehouse and sprinted to the car. After peeking through the window and spotting nothing unusual, she used her spare key to open the driver's side door. Inside was an empty Doritos bag and a half-full can of beer, but no obvious clues that led to Woody. Then a terrible thought occurred to her—he could be stuffed in the trunk. There wasn't much space, but a strong, determined person could do it.

She hesitated to verify her suspicion. Seeing Woody crumpled up and dead would give her no satisfaction whatsoever. And as with the sewer, she didn't want to live with such a vision seared into her memory. But what if he was alive in the trunk and she drove away without checking? She would never forgive herself if her inaction resulted in his death. So she pulled a lever that opened the trunk and then inched around the car to glance at the contents. When she didn't see his body, she was overcome with relief before running to her car for her cell phone. She had to call the Sheriff and let him know that she had found Cricket's car. Maybe he would bring a search party that could locate Woody in the area and end this whole fiasco. She hurriedly dialed the Sheriff's phone number but paused before initiating the call. Now that Fern seemed to be a suspect, Sheriff Pat was unlikely to believe that she had simply happened upon the car. Rather, he would think that Fern knew exactly how the car had gotten here and take her in for questioning. He might even try to put her in jail. While she didn't have Jasmine's legal expertise, she did have a fairly reliable gut instinct. And her gut was telling her to lock up Cricket's car and get the heck outta there without telling anyone what she'd found. So that's exactly what she did.

Chapter 7

B.J. had been watching the house for hours and getting angrier by the second. Aside from Woody's wife and children, there'd been nothing to see—meaning no Woody. He began to wonder if Woody was hiding inside with plans to escape at nightfall. He could have been at home this whole time and told Fern to lie when he'd seen B.J. at the door. The age-old virtue of telling the truth and shaming the devil was flung right out the window in certain situations, and a marital commitment was typically one of them. This was unfortunate since Fern seemed to be an otherwise nice lady. Not bad looking either. She had a bodacious figure that a man could hold onto, beautiful brown eyes that he could drown in. But her brainpower had to be running on empty because no one with a scintilla of intelligence would take up with a bottom-feeder like Woody.

B.J. had had enough of sitting in his truck and waiting for Woody to appear. From the looks of it, everyone was gone, but looks could be deceiving. So he walked to the house and rang the doorbell. No one answered. He went around to the back to peek through a window, but the curtains were drawn on every last one of them. B.J. spat on the ground and stared at the back door. The thought of kicking it in was gaining momentum, but he instead called out Woody's name. Receiving no response, he continued to glare at the door, assessing his options. While he had the means to gain illegal entry to the house, he thought better about being too rash. He could be wrong about Woody being at home, and breaking in would only bring unwanted heat. He pressed an ear against the door and a few windows. All was quiet. It seemed best that he wait for Fern to come back. And the next time she left, he would be on her tail like white on rice until she led him to her gutless husband.

Pat had longstanding relationships with most of the people in town, and it gave him no pleasure to place any of them under arrest. While doing so was at times necessary, the fallout made his presence at town picnics and holiday celebrations unusually touchy. He'd gotten the evil eye more than once from good friends and family members of those he had jailed. It was one of the drawbacks that came with his job, one of those things that he would happily kiss off when he retired.

As it was, he was now called upon to put his friendship with Fern's father on the line. Hiram was a well-liked retired postmaster and army veteran. Although he sometimes came across as a little gruff, he would give the shirt off of his back to someone in need—as long as that someone wasn't named Woody Walker. Because of Hiram's sterling reputation, Pat had always brushed off the rumors about the bad blood between him and Woody. He had assumed that nothing but cross words would come of their hairy relationship. But after speaking with multiple people who recounted Woody's fears that Hiram was going to kill him, Pat had to question whether he had been too generous in his appraisal of Hiram. The simple truth was that once Woody had struck Fern, everything had changed, and it sounded like Hiram had been harassing him ever since. He wished that Woody would've reported these incidents to him before things had escalated to a point where Woody was afraid to sleep at home. More than that, though, he wished that Woody would've kept his hands to himself. An angry parent was capable of almost anything when he believed his child was being abused. And Woody had poked the wrong bear with no one to blame but himself.

With so many people pointing fingers at Hiram, there were questions that had to be asked and answered. And Pat wanted to use a surprise visit to do the asking. Hiram had a roster full of reasons to get rid of Woody, and maybe he had done it with Fern's help—or maybe not. But the longer Woody was missing, the more Fern and her family were looking like suspects rather than merely disgruntled kinfolk.

As he neared Hiram's homestead, Pat waved at a few of his neighbors. Most of the people in this area were empty nesters like him, and they either traveled the globe or carted their grandchildren to events around town. Those who attended Little League games were particularly tight-knit. They were also one of Pat's greatest sources of who did what to whom. Interestingly, not one of them had come forward regarding Woody.

Upon reaching Hiram's house and ringing the doorbell, his wife, Trudy, answered the door. A petite, gray-haired lady, she had stuck by Hiram's side since meeting him in Germany during one of his tours of duty. The product of a military family herself, she had insisted that he retire before they had children because she didn't want to haul them from country to country as she had been. Unquestionably, a lot of strength was packed into Trudy's small body, and she was equally as protective of her children as Hiram.

"Sheriff Pat, I don't believe that we're expecting you, are we?"

"Hello, Trudy. No, I'm afraid that this isn't a social call. I'm here about Woody."

"Oh? Have you found him?"

"Unfortunately, I can't say that I have. I need to speak with Hiram. Is he at home?"

"Of course. Come in." She opened the door wider to allow him entry. "Have a seat while I get him."

"Sure, thank you." Pat did as told and studied the living room while waiting for Hiram. He knew that there was a wooden gun cabinet somewhere in the house with at least ten rifles in it. Had any of them been fired lately?

"Well, this sure is a surprise." Hiram casually walked in, shook Pat's hand, and took a seat next to him as Trudy stood behind him. Contrary to his normal nature, he didn't crack a smile.

"It's good to see you, Hiram."

"Trudy says that you have news about Woody."

"No, I don't have news. I'm here because I have questions about your relationship with Woody. I've talked to multiple people who know him well, and they all say that Woody is afraid of you."

"That's right. And he should be afraid after hitting my daughter. He's a mealymouthed coward."

"Yes, yes, I understand how you feel about him and why. I'm going to come right out and ask you: Did you do anything that has caused his disappearance?"

"Anything like what?" Hiram seemed indignant at the question.

"You tell me. I don't want to put words in your mouth."

"Sheriff, if you drove all the way over here to accuse me of murder, then you've wasted your time and gas. I don't have anything to tell you. None of us know where Woody is or whether he's six feet under."

"But you're hoping that he's dead, aren't you?" Pat attempted to bait him into revealing his guilt.

"I wouldn't care if he is, but I don't know that he is."

"Sheriff," Trudy interjected, "how we feel about Woody doesn't matter. The man is missing and needs to be found. He has a family that needs him."

"I agree with you. And I'm sure that you believe that, but your husband is a different story. I've gotten more than an earful about him threatening Woody. And I heard that Woody is too scared to even sleep in his own house because Hiram might go by and kill him."

"That's preposterous!"

"It's Fern's house," Hiram clarified. "Woody is nothing more than a squatter."

"Again, I understand how you feel about him. And I'd feel the same way if I were in your shoes."

"Damned right you would!"

"I'm not denying it. I won't insult your intelligence. But I need to know what happened to him, and your grudge against him has forced me to look at you."

"As a suspect?"

"As a person of interest. I'm just being honest with you."

Trudy gasped as Hiram coolly sustained eye contact with Pat. "Sheriff, as much as I can't stand that sniveling snot, I have not harmed one hair on his head. However, it does my heart well every time I hear that he's terrified of me. I eat it up like a hungry wolf."

"That's an interesting choice of animal. Not the most genteel."

"Not known to attack unprovoked either."

Pat nodded, his suspicions undiminished. "Can you tell me where you were Friday night between the hours of nine o'clock and let's say around eight o'clock the next morning?"

"I was right here at home."

"He sure was. He was here with me all night," Trudy readily confirmed.

"Have you used any of your rifles lately? Or loaned any out to someone who wanted to use them?"

"No. All of my rifles are locked in the cabinet where they always are. None of them have been fired since I stopped hunting deer a few years ago."

"Hiram has had to cut down on his meat."

"I see. So have I." Pat paused and frowned. "I may as well tell you that Fern is high on my list of potential suspects in Woody's disappearance."

"And just why the hell would that be?" Hiram was immediately fired up as Trudy gasped again.

"She's one of the last people who saw Woody, and spouses are always suspects when one of them turns up dead."

"But Woody isn't dead."

"Well, not that we know of. But he's been missing for four days, and that's a mighty bad sign."

"Maybe he's so scared of me that he tucked his tail and left town. Did you think about that?"

"Or maybe he didn't leave town. Maybe someone killed him."

"If he's dead, it wouldn't be Fern who did it, Sheriff. That dog don't hunt. Why, he's so stupid that he could've accidentally killed himself."

"With what? One of your rifles?"

"He has never laid a finger on any of my rifles. But he could've tripped and fallen off the bridge on Highway 95. He could be floating in a river downstream by now, bloated and blue."

"Could be."

"You should look into that."

"What do you think the chances are that we'll find him in the river?" Pat continued to try to rope Hiram into an unintentional confession.

"Better than you pinning a murder on my daughter." Hiram stood up, at which point Pat took his cue to do the same. "I've always liked you, Pat. And I know you have a job to do, but I'm done answering your questions. I think you should leave."

"I'm sorry that we had to have this conversation. And I want you to know that I'll do everything in my power to conduct this investigation as fairly and objectively as possible. One way or another, I'm going to find out where Woody is."

"And I want you to know that if you try to arrest my daughter, you won't have one leg to stand on by the time I'm through."

"What does that mean?"

"It means that I protect my own. And you're not the only one with a bag of tricks." Hiram headed for the front door as Pat followed in a state of consternation.

"Are you threatening me, Hiram? I sure hope you're not because that wouldn't be a good idea."

Hiram opened the door and stepped aside for Pat to pass him. "I've lived my life, Sheriff, but Fern has barely started hers. I will not allow you to ruin it."

"I'm not out to ruin anyone's life. All I'm trying to do is the job that people like yourself are paying me to do. If someone's life is ruined because I've done my job, then they have only themselves to blame."

"I've said all that I'm going to say. The next time that you want to speak to me, you'll have to call my attorney."

"Huh. All right then." He glanced at Trudy and nodded politely before exiting the home, having gotten little of what he'd come for. Hiram's denial about killing Woody had been both convincing and truthful as far as Pat could tell. He'd paid close attention and seen no indications of deception. But this wasn't enough to scratch Hiram off of his list of suspects. Pat opened his car door and turned to face Hiram and Trudy, who were standing together, a united front, in the doorway. Pat asked one last, critical question as though it was an afterthought. "By the way, do either of you know if Woody was into drugs?"

The pair exchanged puzzled looks.

"No," Hiram replied. "Why?"

"Just covering all the bases." He got into his car, discouraged. Two days in, and he still didn't know diddly-squat. Hopefully, the lab results for the pills would give him something concrete to go on. They might even justify a request for the Texas Rangers to assist with his investigation. Until he got them, every lead, no matter how small or unlikely, had to be delved into. So he radioed one of his deputies named Chip and ordered him to check the river for a body.

Fern was so frazzled at finding Cricket's car that she should've called in sick instead of going to work that evening. But with her bank account balance nearing zero, she was obliged to soldier on and so strolled into the diner with her mouth sealed shut about the car. Being among her most loyal allies without letting her tongue fly would be a monumental task, but confiding in them wouldn't be wise. She feared that they might slip when the Sheriff returned to finish questioning everyone. And though they all had good intentions, their intentions wouldn't bail her out of jail.

Tonight, Gail and Deedee shared her shift, and they were on her heels as soon as they saw her.

"Have you heard anything about Woody yet?" Deedee stood at Fern's side as she placed her purse inside her locker.

"No, not yet. The Sheriff is looking for him."

"We heard." Gail shook her head sympathetically. "Jared said that he was here this morning asking questions. I don't know what he expects any of us to say. It's not like we ever see Woody."

"He's trying to find out if I did something to him."

"Something like what?"

"Like killed him."

"Shut your mouth!"

"That's what he's got in his head." Fern wearily tied her apron around her waist.

"Well...did you?" Gail's eyes widened. Although in her forties, she had managed to hang on to a childlike innocence that was equal to that of a seventh grader. But such innocence didn't extend to her plump hips and breasts, which strained the seams of her uniform. Needless to say, she was a main attraction for many male customers.

"Of course she didn't." Deedee slapped Gail's arm with a napkin she was holding.

"No, I didn't. He took off in Cricket's car, and that's all I know. I'm just as baffled as everyone else."

"Pat has some nerve coming around here, trying to make you look like a criminal. I'd like to put him over my knee and spank him like a naughty boy."

"Pretty as you are, he'd probably like that." Fern smiled weakly at Deedee's protective instincts.

"Is there anything that we can do to help you? How are you feeling?"

"Dog-tired and wired up at the same time. I've racked my mind trying to figure where Woody could be. And my kids are scared to death about what may have happened to him." Fern heaved a great sigh as they filed back to the front of the diner, back to their work. "I'm afraid that Woody was into something that he had no business in. The Sheriff found drugs under our bed when he searched the house, enough to kill an elephant."

"Drugs? Where in the world would Woody get drugs?" Gail's disbelief was palpable. Behind them, they heard a customer begin to call for service. "Shoot, I've gotta get back to work. We can finish talking later."

She hugged Fern tightly before strutting away as Deedee's face contorted into an expression of absolute confusion.

"How could Woody be doing drugs without you knowing?"

"It wouldn't be too hard, I guess. I hardly see him. I work at night and sleep while he's up during the day. Really and truly, I just..." Fern shrugged with exasperation. "I just don't know what to think."

Deedee placed a comforting hand on Fern's shoulder. "The Sheriff shouldn't be so quick to assume that you killed him. Whatever has happened, Woody brought it on himself."

"I know. And to make matters worse, a man the size of a gorilla came by the house this morning looking for him. As soon as I saw him, I knew that Woody was in big trouble. It's probably best that he stay gone."

"My Lord in heaven! You'd better tell the Sheriff about him, Fern. What if he's a drug addict or a dealer? You don't know what he might do if he can't find Woody."

"I thought about that, but I've decided to get an attorney before talking to Pat anymore. He's already made up his mind, and nothing I say is going to change that." Fern was watching the entrance and suddenly bristled. "What do ya know? Speak of the devil."

Pat was standing near the hostess station. When he saw Fern, he simply nodded an acknowledgment.

"I guess that he's not here to see me."

"I still think you should talk to him."

Fern shook her head.

"Then I'll go find out what he wants." Deedee haughtily marched over to the Sheriff, who didn't seem interested in being seated. After a brief conversation, Deedee walked back toward Fern and said, "He wants to see Bernie."

As she left to find their boss, Fern grabbed a tablet and went to her first customer's table. "Hi there, Lionel." She tried to focus on him, but one of her eyes followed every move the Sheriff made.

"How are you doing, Fern?"

"As well as I can be under the circumstances. I assume that you've heard about Woody."

"Everyone has. Bad news travels fast. We're all praying that Woody'll come back soon." He gestured to Sheriff Dupree. "Don't usually see him here so late in the day. I heard he's looking for Woody."

"Yep, he's looking, but he's not here for any good reason."

"Why do you say that?"

"Because he's decided that I'm his prime suspect in Woody's disappearance. He thinks that I killed him."

"That's hogwash! What gave him such a crazy idea?"

"If I knew, I'd tell you. He's beating the bushes, though. Been asking my coworkers questions about me."

"What kind of questions?"

"Oh, stuff about my mood the night Woody went missing and whether I left work. He's trying to figure out if I had an opportunity to kill him. The good Lord already knows that I have plenty of reasons to."

"You and a lot of other people in town. I heard that Woody stole somebody's dog and sold it for cash."

"That can't be right. Someone would've told me about it."

"I don't think so."

"Why not?"

"Because the dog belongs to a woman of ill repute. And nobody wants to hurt your feelings more than they already are."

Fern's brow crinkled. "Who is she?"

"I'll tell you only because it might help you get the Sheriff off your back."

"Who, Lionel?"

"A lady by the name of Shasta. I don't know her last name, but she's—"

"I know who she is." Fern shook her head to herself. Suddenly, everything was starting to make sense. All the nights that Woody wasn't at home when she called to check on the kids, the money that he'd withdrawn from their bank account before she'd cut him off. "A prostitute. That son of a gun was using my hard-earned money to pay for a prostitute."

"You didn't hear it from me."

"Damn him." She huffed loudly. "When did he steal her dog?"

"I'm not sure, but I heard about it a couple of weeks ago. She got it back, but it cost her a pretty penny. I hear that she's the type who would've gotten revenge for that. She's from Louisiana, and those people are into voodoo. Geraldine says that one of her chickens is gone, and she thinks that Shasta took it, but she can't prove it."

"My word!" She saw Bernie walk over to Sheriff Dupree, at which point they stepped outside where no one could overhear their conversation. "Lionel, has the Sheriff questioned you about me?"

"No, why would he?"

"Because you were here the night that Woody disappeared."

"So?"

"So he might want to know what you saw and heard." She didn't want to verbalize her exact concerns. It was possible that he hadn't seen or heard anything that could put her behind bars.

"To the best of my knowledge, Fern, he hasn't spoken to any of Bernie's customers."

"Well, if he did speak with you, what would you tell him? What do you remember about that night?"

"I'd tell him that you were as kind as you always are." He smiled at her.

Filled with immeasurable gratitude, Fern patted his shoulder. "Thank you, Lionel. That's very sweet." She looked back toward the front door and saw Bernie come back inside and wave at her.

"Hold on. Bernie wants something. I'll be right back." She reluctantly trod the short distance to him. "Yes, sir?"

"Sheriff Dupree is here to ask my staff some questions. He says that he'll speak to you last but not to worry. He's following a standard protocol."

"Standard my foot. I've tried to reach him at least fifty times today, and never once did he return my call. I don't trust him, Bernie. I think he's up to something."

"Y'all just tell him the truth, and I'm sure that you'll have nothing to worry about. You want him to find Woody, don't you?" He dashed off before she could answer.

Soon after, Gail passed by on her way to the Sheriff's vehicle, quickly squeezing Fern's hand before exiting the diner.

Chapter 8

People like Woody didn't run off without telling somebody where they were going. As Calvin had stated, a free ride was hard to come by and—for better or worse—Woody had found one in Fern. Pat surmised that she had finally snapped. It wouldn't've surprised anyone. But she would've needed help to get rid of a body as rotund as Woody's, which is where a trusted family member would've stepped in. Any of them would've been more than happy to lend a helping hand. The stick in Pat's craw, though, was the pills. Woody's drug-related affairs were just as likely as Fern's malice to be the reason he'd been wiped clean off the face of the earth. Oddly, no one had bothered to tell Pat about Woody's illicit escapade, and something just didn't feel right. Then it hit him—maybe the drugs weren't Woody's at all. Maybe Fern had planted the pills under the bed so that Pat would find them and spend all his time chasing his own tail. He'd seen how meticulous her housecleaning was. What was the likelihood that a woman who was so thorough with washing, mopping, and dusting never looked under her own bed? When he thought of it that way, it seemed plausible that Fern had set him up. More importantly, she'd successfully relieved herself of Woody.

Pat scratched his head, struggling to make the puzzle pieces fit. But the more he tried, the more he realized that he could easily let his imagination get away from him. Rather than dwelling on conjecture, he sent one of his deputies, Lester, to the town's hotbed of addicts and pushers to probe the drug angle. If Woody had ever shown his face in those parts, Pat needed someone to blab. In the meantime, he would finish questioning the waitstaff at Bernie's diner despite having slim to no chance at getting the truth out of any of them. Knowing that Gail wasn't too sharp, he would start with her.

When she came outside, Pat opened the passenger door of his car like a perfect gentleman, and closed it after she was comfortably seated. He was going to treat her like fine China, the idea being to lower her guard. Once he got back into the car, the first thing he noticed was that it was filled with the scent of her perfume—and he didn't like it one bit. "That sure is a nice fragrance that you're wearing. Mind telling me what brand it is so I can get it for Ellie?"

"Thank you! It's La Fleur by Joubert. Heard of it?"

"Not until now, but I'll be buying a bottle real soon."

"That's nice. I'm sure that Ellie will love it."

"I think so, too." He brought out his notepad and stifled a cough. "Gail, as everyone knows by now, Fern's husband, Woody, is missing."

"Yes, it's so sad. And I feel so sorry for her kids."

"It's an awful situation for everyone, especially them. That's why I'm working so hard to find him. We've got to bring him back home and back to his children. Nothing matters more than that."

"I agree, Sheriff. He might be the biggest jerk in town, but he's still their father."

"That's right. And in the name of restoring him to his children, I want you to be as candid with me as humanly possible."

"Oh, I will, Sheriff. I'll tell you whatever you need to know."

"I appreciate that. I'd like to start with anything you may know about Woody personally. When was the last time you saw him?"

"It's been a good while. He used to drop by the diner for a free dinner when Fern was at work. But that all stopped at least a year ago."

"Why did he stop coming?"

"Because Fern told him that he had to. His free meals were actually coming out of her paycheck, and she just couldn't afford to keep feeding him like that. She'd gone along with it only to keep the peace at home, but then he hit her, and the wheels came off."

"I see." He jotted down her comments. "Has Fern been angry with Woody since he hit her?"

"I'd say so. Who wouldn't be?"

"Angry enough to want him gone?"

"Maybe at times. All they do is argue. And on top of that, he's a deadbeat. She wouldn't be losing anything if he left, but those kids...well, they love him to death. He can't do any wrong in their eyes."

Pat scribbled more notes. "Has Fern ever said anything about harming Woody?"

"Oh sure. She's talked about beating him with a bat if she could." Gail chuckled, nearly causing her bountiful bosom to bounce out of her uniform. "But she didn't mean anything by it. She was just blowing off steam. All of my married friends have thought about beating their husbands on account of something they've done. It's just talk."

"Did she make these types of comments more frequently after Woody hit her?"

"Maybe. I don't pay much attention to it."

So far, their discussion had been amicable, and Pat was satisfied that Gail was being forthright. She'd even shared new details about Fern's violent inclinations toward Woody. "What do you know about the night that Woody went missing?"

"Not much. Fern had to leave early, so Carlos called me to fill in for her. She was already gone when I got here."

"Do you know why she left?"

"Jared said that Woody had called, and Fern flew out of here like a bat out of hell."

Now they were getting somewhere. "Did Jared say where Fern was going?"

"He didn't know, but..." Her words trailed off, and it seemed that Gail had changed her mind about finishing her statement.

"But what?"

"Maybe I shouldn't say." She appeared to be getting flustered. "I think I've already said too much."

"You can tell me, Gail," Pat reassured her as calmly as he could. "Remember, we need to bring Woody home to his children. That's what all of this is about."

"I'm sorry, Sheriff, but I don't think I should keep talking. Fern says that you're out to get her, and I don't want any part of that."

"Out to get her? Why would she think that?"

"Because you've been asking a lot of questions about her and Woody, making it seem like she murdered him or something. Fern says that she didn't do anything to him but you think she did."

The chitchat train had been abruptly derailed, and Pat was going to have to use supreme finesse to get it back on track. "Fern is wrong about me, Gail. The only thing that I'm out to get is the truth. And I think that you and I both care about the truth, right? You're a God-fearing woman. I know you are. And I'm a God-fearing man. The truth is my compass, and I'm going to go wherever it tells me to go because that's my job. If Fern is innocent, the compass is going to point me away from her. But I need your help to point me in the right direction."

He could see that his pep talk had made headway, but just as Gail opened her mouth to speak again, someone started banging on his window. Gail practically jumped out of her skin as Pat turned around and saw Fern's angry face. He rolled down the window, peeved that she had ruined the breakthrough he had almost accomplished. "Didn't Bernie tell you that I was going to speak with you later?"

"Didn't Dottie tell you that I tried to reach you this morning? Why haven't you returned any of my calls?"

"I've been busy, but I can talk to you in around an hour. Go back inside, and wait until then."

"I'll do no such thing. I happen to have important information about Woody."

He groaned and glanced at Gail, who had completely clammed up. He wouldn't be getting anything else from her today. "Gail, you can go back to work. Thank you for talking to me." As Gail fled the car, his cell phone rang, so he mechanically grabbed it from the cupholder. "Yes, Chip. What is it?"

"Sheriff, I was on the way to the river when I passed by the abandoned warehouse that Coors used to own. And that missing car—the one that Mrs. Walker reported stolen—is parked in plain sight."

"You're kidding."

"No, sir. I'm looking at it right now."

"Any way to find out how long it's been there?" Pat knew the area was desert land with the exception of the warehouse.

"No, sir. The security cameras on the warehouse are inoperable."

"Damn. You didn't try to open the doors, did you?"

"No, but I did look through the windows. Didn't see anything unusual."

"Okay. Call Odell and tell her to meet me at the warehouse as soon as possible." Odell was the town's one and only crime scene investigator.

"Should I go on to the river?"

"Wait until I get there. Should be around thirty minutes."

"Sir, it'll be too dark to see much in thirty minutes."

"Well, you can go tomorrow morning then. First thing."

"Yes, sir."

While Pat had been talking to Chip, Fern had taken Gail's place in the car. When he set his phone back down, he faced her with no intention of sharing Chip's news. "What have you got to tell me, Fern?"

"I think the first question is what have you got for me? I've been waiting to hear what you found out about those pills in the shoebox."

"Nothing yet. I'm expecting the lab's call real soon."

"They sure are slow. Why does it take so long?"

"They handle more cases than just ours, and murders come first."

"Oh. I guess that makes sense."

He sighed grumpily. "What else?"

"I thought you'd want to know that Woody has been seeing a prostitute in town named Shasta."

"I've heard of her."

"Have you also heard that Woody stole her dog and sold it earlier this month?"

"Who told you that?"

"I'd rather not say, but if it's true, you need to be investigating Shasta. She's from Louisiana and knows how to use voodoo."

Pat was skeptical of the rumor since he'd just seen Shasta with her dog earlier that day. "That would be a wild goose chase. I happen to know that Shasta has her dog as we speak."

"That's because she bought it back from whoever got it from Woody. I heard it cost her a lot of money, too."

"How did she find the buyer?"

"I don't know! The point is that she had an ax to grind with Woody. And now nobody knows where he is. Don't you think that the timing is a little too coincidental?"

"Could be, could be."

"What do you mean, 'could be'? This woman may have killed my husband. Aren't you going to check it out?"

"Yes, you can be sure of it."

"Good." She opened the car door and put one leg out. "And another thing. There's a whopper-sized man named B.J. in town looking for Woody. Have you seen him yet?"

"What does B.J. look like?"

"Like a refrigerator. He's tall and muscular, could be in his early forties. You can't miss him."

"I haven't seen any strangers who fit that description."

"You should find him and check him out, too. He came to my house this morning and scared the bejesus out of me."

"Why? Did he threaten you?"

"No, but when I told him that Woody wasn't at home, he looked like he wanted to rip my face off. I half expected him to barge inside to see if I was lying. If you can find out why he wants to see Woody, you might find out why Woody is missing. Maybe the drugs you found belong to B.J."

Pat couldn't say what he was thinking, but he would not be led around by any carrots that she dangled in front of him. He didn't know anything about this B.J. guy or whether he even existed. What he did know was that Fern had every reason in the world to distract him from his present occupation. "Did he tell you where he's staying?"

"No, but he did say that he'll be coming back to the house, which I'm afraid could be anytime soon."

"Okay, I'll ask Dottie to call all the hotels to find him, and then I'll go see him. Is there anyone else you think I should talk to?"

Her eyes narrowed. "Why do you have to be so sarcastic?"

"I'm not being sarcastic. All I said was—"

"I heard what you said, and you said it sarcastically." Fern jumped out of the car and slammed the door with radioactive fury before leaning down to peer at him through the window. "I know you think that I killed Woody, but you're wrong. There's more people than I can shake a stick at who could've done something to him, but noooo. The only head you want is mine."

"Fern, I assure you that I'm talking to everyone and running down every lead. Don't you worry about that."

"Well, I can't tell, and neither can anyone else."

Pat put his vehicle in gear. "I can't discuss an open investigation with you, but we can talk about all of your theories when I come back."

"No thank you, Sheriff. From now on, you can just talk to my attorney."

She stormed back inside the restaurant as Pat's brows furrowed. His job would be much harder now that she and Hiram had lawyered up. And the fact was that those who hired lawyers were usually guilty of something. He wasn't supposed to see it that way, but history spoke for itself.

As he drove to the warehouse, Pat realized that he had no choice but to further broaden his scope. While his sights were logically set on Fern and her family, he would be off his rocker if he didn't take a closer look at Shasta. She was hardly above reproach. If it was true that Woody had stolen her dog, Pat could read all kinds of bad tidings into her failure to mention it when they'd spoken. And given that she'd casually reeled off a list of methods to covertly kill someone, their whole conversation would be cast in a new light. If it wasn't true, then Fern may have concocted the story to send him down another rabbit hole. And all things considered, this would be par for the course. The bottom line was that he would be paying another visit to Shasta.

The warehouse came into sight as Dottie's voice erupted from the CB. "Sheriff, are you there?"

He crankily picked up the receiver. "Yep, I'm here. Almost at the warehouse."

"We finally heard from the lab about those pills, and you'll never believe the results."

"What are they? Uppers, downers?"

"Neither. They're Tylenol."

"Tylenol? There's no Tylenol logo on them. I would've seen that right off."

"The lab says that someone crushed the tablets into powder and then used superglue to harden them back up."

"Superglue? Why the heck would anyone do that?"

"To pass them off as street drugs, Sheriff. The lab thinks that the pills look real similar to PCP."

"PCP," he repeated to himself, letting it sink in.

"That's right. PCP. And if Woody sold them to the wrong types, we might not ever find him. His body could be scattered all over creation by now. And the coyotes would've been glad for it."

"Hmm. Did the lab dust the box for fingerprints?"

"Of course. They only got matches for Woody." Thanks to his arrest last year, Woody's prints were in the national database. "They also checked all the plastic pill packages. Nobody but Woody touched them."

Pat winced at the findings. They had set his investigation back at square one. They had also ruled out a request for assistance from the Texas Rangers.

"You gonna go to Mercury Street? That's where most of his customers would be."

"I might. I'm waiting to hear from Lester." He sighed with disgust. It had been a long day, and after hours of investigating, this is what it had come to—a longer list of suspects, most of them nameless. If Woody had indeed slung phony drugs and lived to talk about it, he surely had every swindled addict in town after him. Not to mention the pushers who didn't take kindly to competitors invading their territories. If the muck had hit the fan, who was Woody most likely to run to? None other than Calvin and Roy. So in addition to Shasta, Pat had to speak with them again. And this time, he was going to come down hard because one or all of them had lied about what they knew.

"One more thing, Sheriff. Liddie called for an update on your investigation. What should I tell her?"

"Tell her that I'll call her tonight after I leave the warehouse. Don't tell her where I am. Just tell her that I'll call her."

"You got it."

"After that, I need you to call the media. Let's get Woody on tonight's news as a missing person." The town's biggest weapon was its prying eyes and ears. But Pat used it sparingly since he would be flooded with every type of conspiracy theory. These were truly desperate times.

"Should they use his mug shot?"

"Just the neck up. No inmate ID numbers in the photo. And before I forget, call all the hotels in town until you find a gentleman who either goes by the name B.J. or has a first and last name with those initials. He may be important to the case."

"I'm on it."

Pat slumped, feeling like the wind had been taken out of his sails. He pulled into the warehouse parking lot and greeted Chip, an all-American model of Hercules. While Chip stood guard over Cricket's car, Odell used a flashlight to see into crevices as the sun began to set. A heavyset, serious woman in her thirties, she ignored all attempts at humor, rendering them a lost cause.

"Have you found anything of interest, Odell?" Pat asked.

She withdrew a gloved hand from the car and stood up straight upon hearing his voice. "I found these under the passenger seat." She held up a few packets of yellow pills. "They look like PCP or maybe a bad batch of heroin. You think the daughter is dealing?"

He scowled at the pills. "No, I think we have a missing person who a lot of people want dead. Chip, call Leonard and Miguel. We need to search the vicinity for Woody's body."

Chapter 9

Later that evening, the phone at Bernie's Bistro was ringing nonstop as boatloads of customers streamed in to inquire about Woody's disappearance. Through them, Fern discovered that the story had hit the news, kicking the town's rumor mill into high gear. To her shock, she also heard that several people had recently seen Woody near his favorite bar, claims that made her heart skip a beat with cautious relief. Noisy chatter engulfed the diner, eventually causing Bernie to send Fern home early. He said that paying customers weren't receiving proper attention because her head was in the clouds. Although she wasn't happy with his decision, she packed it in knowing that this month's cash flow was going to be extra tight. On the bright side, though, at least she had reason to hope that Pat would finally get off of her back. That man had proven to be as stubborn as a mule. And Fern had lost control of herself when he'd chosen Gail for his first interrogation. His strategy to pick off the weakest among them had been so transparent that rage had literally blown her out the door to sabotage his scheme. And judging by Gail's face, Fern's intrusion had been none too soon. She'd looked like a trapped rat trying to find her way out of a maze, fanning the flames of Fern's fury. In that moment, her fear of being arrested had come second to her urge to give Pat a piece of her mind—and, of course, to share the tidbits about Shasta and B.J. Seeing as how he was a dog in need of a bone, he could go fetch those two.

"Chew on them long and hard, Sheriff," she muttered to herself as she vacuumed her bedroom the following morning. "And while you're at it, chew on all the rumors that Woody is alive somewhere." But where? The question hung in her mind like wet laundry on a line that was flailing in the wind. Where in the world could he be? And why was he staying away from home? Was it because of B.J.? The drugs? Shasta? She didn't know the what or the who, but she did know one thing—Calvin and Roy were holding out. They were protecting Woody and themselves from something, and Fern wanted to know what that something was. The time had come for her to stop waiting around for Pat to find a reason to handcuff her while those two did everything in their power to send her up the river. Starting now, she was going to take her life into her own hands.

Once again fired up, she left the house and was backing out of her driveway when her cell phone rang. It was Jasmine.

"Hey, Daddy told me that you need a lawyer, and I'm calling to let you know that Consuela Iglesias has agreed to represent you both. I've already informed Dottie so she can tell the Sheriff."

"Thanks, but what do you mean by 'both'?"

"I mean you and Daddy. Didn't he tell you?"

"Tell me what?"

"The Sheriff went by the house yesterday and told Daddy and Mama that you and he are suspects in his investigation."

"No! He—no!" Fern was outraged. "Why Daddy?"

"Girl, you know why. Come on. The whole town knows why, and I'm not so sure that they're wrong."

"Why not?"

"Are you really going to play stupid with me? As long as Daddy has been talking about killing Woody, you don't think he could've done it?"

"No, I don't think that. I can't think that."

"Well, I can. I'm not saying that he did it, but it wouldn't surprise me if he did."

"No, Jasmine, no. No, no, no. I don't believe that. No." Fern had been so wrapped up in protecting herself that she'd failed to realize that her father was also a sitting duck. "Is he okay?"

"He's fine. You know Daddy. He's more concerned about you than he is about himself."

"Oh God." Fern nearly broke down in tears as she drove out of her neighborhood toward Roy's house. "There's literally a witch in town practicing voodoo under everyone's noses and boning Woody. But who does Pat go after? Innocent people who are living honest lives."

"Yeah, I heard about Shasta yesterday and told Consuela. She's got to be put under a microscope if Pat is doing his job."

"Who told you about Shasta?"

"June Bug spilled the beans when he saw Woody on the news. He said that Shasta took one of his sister's chickens to put a hex on Woody."

"Does he know that for sure?"

"He can't prove it, but that's what they think."

"Gawd."

"Consuela's going to call you this morning to discuss your case and where things stand now that Cricket's car was located. I assume that you haven't heard about that yet."

"No, I haven't. Where'd they find it?" Fern was still determined to maintain a pretense of utter ignorance, but she'd gathered that this was coming while sitting in Pat's car yesterday. She'd overheard just enough of his phone conversation.

"At the old Coors warehouse outside of town last night. Consuela will fill you in on the details, but the most important thing is that Woody is still missing. They searched the whole area and didn't find so much as a sock."

She bit her lip hard enough to draw blood. "So, what's next?"

"They're going to examine the car from top to bottom, and then Cricket will probably get it back."

"Then what? What about Woody?"

"They'll keep looking for him. But to be honest with you, they're not optimistic that they'll find him. They got the lab results for the pills, which, by the way, it would've been nice if you'd told me about them."

"Augh!" Fern slapped her forehead. "I forgot to. Everything has been so crazy."

"I understand, but the pills turned out to be a curveball. They were made of Tylenol and superglue. Nothing illegal in 'em."

"That great!"

"It's great as long as he wasn't using the pills to run scams on people who thought that they were buying something stronger like PCP. Right now, nobody knows what to make of 'em."

Fern slammed the breaks. "My God. That explains the man who came to the house looking for Woody yesterday. He must've bought some of those pills, and now he wants to kill him."

"What man? Who are you talking about?"

"A sasquatch named B.J. I already told the Sheriff about him." She cupped her mouth with her hand. "If he finds Woody before the cops do—oh my God. Oh my God." Her voice trembled at the thought of what B.J. could do to Woody with his bare hands.

"Calm down. We don't know if anything has happened to Woody, so don't get ahead of yourself. When you speak to Consuela, tell her about B.J. so she can put one of her investigators on him."

"Okay," Fern croaked before hitting the gas again, still shaken.

"Everything's going to be all right, Fern. Try to get some rest."

"Yeah, right." They exchanged goodbyes, and Fern glumly rubbed her eyes. They were toting a hefty set of luggage that was darkening by the hour. But despite her sister's parting advice, rest was the last thing on her mind. She was compelled by a much stronger need to know what Roy knew. Now more than ever, she had to know where Woody was.

When she turned onto Roy's street, she realized that someone in a police car was driving straight toward her. "What the—"

Both cars soon reached Roy's driveway and stopped bumper-to-bumper, whereupon Fern stared through her windshield at the other driver—Sheriff Pat. He immediately got out of his car and barreled toward her, foaming at the mouth.

"Why are you here?" His face had turned beet red.

"Why are you here?"

"That's police business."

"I'm entitled to know if it has anything to do with Woody."

"Call your attorney and leave so that I can do my job."

"I'm not leaving, and you can't make me."

"Damn it, Fern, why do you have to be so difficult? I don't want to arrest you for interfering with a police investigation, but you're really pushing me."

"You can't do that."

"I can and I will if you don't leave right now." He touched the handcuffs attached to his belt.

She glared at him and pursed her lips while angrily backing up her car. The smell of burning rubber wafted into the air before she shifted back to drive and peeled off. If she'd run over his foot, she wouldn't've been sorry about it. She was sick and tired of men steamrolling her, and this time was going to be the last.

Sitting and waiting had begun to grate on B.J., who had come to town thinking that he would quickly drop the hammer on

Woody and go back home. As that plan had hit the skids, his time was spent listening to the radio, during which he gleaned that the culture in Luna was decidedly slow-paced. Compared to large cities, news about shootings and robberies was sparse, making it easy for him to understand why the citizens enjoyed living here. He also realized that strangers like him would stick out like sore thumbs. For this reason, he couldn't expect to stay put for much longer without someone asking who he was and why he was sleeping in his truck. He was going to have to make a move even if the moment wasn't ideal.

While eating his morning breakfast of beef jerky, he heard the reports about Woody missing and nearly choked. This explained why the bastard hadn't shown his nose around the house. But B.J. didn't believe for one second that Woody had actually vanished. The timing was way too convenient since he'd known that B.J. was coming. It seemed that Woody had gone to great lengths to put himself out of reach, which in turn meant that B.J. needed to change his tactics. His sitting and waiting would have to be upgraded to physical confrontations—and unfortunately for Fern, she was first in line.

At that very moment, he was cruising behind her, keeping a light foot on the gas to avoid being conspicuous. Her driving was erratic, probably because she was on her phone and distracted. He wondered if she was talking to Woody and on her way to his hideout. If so, this could be B.J.'s best chance to corner him, a tantalizing thought that curbed his impulse to head her off and put the fear of God in her.

They reached a neighborhood of pricey homes, at which point B.J. hung back even farther. Not in a million years would he have thought to look for Woody in this area. The idea that he was living high on the hog while B.J. was buried in bills gave him heartburn. It also intensified his grievance. Suddenly, the level of punishment that seemed to be in order would put Woody in the morgue instead of the hospital.

After Fern turned onto a street named Bonnyville, B.J. came to a full stop. There was a police car coming from the opposite direction, and B.J. knew that his beat-up truck would draw the officer's eye. From a safe distance, he watched as Fern exchanged words with the cop before speeding off, not realizing that she'd ditched B.J. But perhaps this was just as well because B.J. wanted to know who was in the house that she'd intended to visit. She'd changed her mind after running into the cop, and he could think of a good reason for that—she was hiding something or someone inside. There was only one way to find out.

B.J. parked his truck and waited as the cop stood at the front door. One way or another, B.J. was going to get inside and go through every room with a fine-tooth comb.

Along with his crew, Pat had spent most of the night searching the warehouse grounds with no reward for the effort. Not only was he frustrated, but he was primed for a fight as he drove to Roy's house. Today he was going to get answers even if he had to use the full force of the law to get them.

On seeing Fern approaching the house, his temper had gotten away from him. There was no good reason for her to be there, and he didn't want her in his way. After running her off, he rang the doorbell multiple times, impatient for someone to answer. Finally, Roy opened the door and peered out with bloodshot eyes, looking like something that the cat had dragged in. He'd clearly had an all-night love affair with a bottle of something strong. "Hello there, Sheriff. Back so soon?"

Pat was in no mood for pleasantries. "Mind if I come in?"

"Sure." He waved Pat inside and left him to close the door. "I was just having a nap by the pool."

"Is anyone else at home?"

"Naw, everyone's gone." He passed through the patio doors and reclined in the same lounge chair that he had occupied two days ago. "Have you arrested Mr. Bennett yet? I heard he confessed to killing Woody."

"Where'd you hear that?"

"Mr. Hawkins told my dad when they played golf yesterday."

"And who told him?"

"His wife, I guess. Is it true? I told you that he'd done it. Wish I could get a reward for my tip." He reached for a glass filled with a clear liquid that surely wasn't water.

"Your tip wasn't worth a three-dollar bill."

"Is that right?"

"That's what I said." Roy looked as though he could nod off at any second, and Pat knew that a strong arm would be pointless. He was sorry that he'd come. "When we spoke a couple of days ago, I asked if Woody was involved with drugs."

"I don't recall that, but I'm sure I would've said that he wasn't. And I would know since he's like a brother to me. Woody's just not that type of guy."

"And what about you? Are you that type of guy?"

"Of course not, Sheriff. Look at me." He appeared to be wearing nothing more than a bathrobe and tighty-whities. "Do I look like I would be a drug dealer?"

"I didn't say anything about drug dealing, Roy."

"I just assumed that that's what you meant."

"I don't believe you. I think you know something that you're not telling me, and it's time for you to talk. Where is Woody?"

"I've already told you everything I know."

Pat noticed that Roy had stopped making eye contact with him. Instead, he looked straight ahead and took bigger swigs from his glass, two glaring hints that he was lying. "I've got a video of you and Woody buying twenty bottles of Tylenol from Walgreens last month." It was a boldfaced lie, but Pat wanted to see Roy's reaction. "Why would you need so much medication? Tell me the truth."

"I don't remember that."

"Then let me jog your memory. Come on down to the station to see the video. Let's go."

"That won't be necessary." He smirked wryly and looked up at Pat. "You could tell me that I had rolled around in pig shit, and I wouldn't remember it. My memory is shot, Sheriff, and seeing myself on a video won't change that."

"But you're not denying it?"

"I can't deny what I don't remember. Maybe I had a bad hangover and Woody was trying to help me."

"It was Tylenol for head colds, not pain."

"Oh, okay, whatever." In his stupor, Roy's words were increasingly slurred together. This was going nowhere.

"Can I take a look around?"

"Help yourself."

Pat had the distinct feeling that he'd be wasting his time. Nevertheless, he took advantage of Roy's permission to search the house and checked under every couch, sofa cushion, bed, and pillow. Then he looked inside every nook and cranny of each room, giving particular attention to Roy's bedroom and bathroom. Unfortunately, the worst he found were empty bottles of alcohol scattered across his closet floor. Had Pat turned up even a smidgeon of marijuana, he would've hauled Roy in on possession charges to shock him back to reality. Stuck with nothing, Pat would have to move on to Calvin, who was next on his hit list.

Pat went back outside where Roy was so still that he appeared to be dead. All that had changed was that his glass was now drained. "I'm going to ask you one last time. Why did you buy twenty bottles of Tylenol? Before you answer me, take a minute to think about Woody. He could be in real danger, and I'm the only one who can help him."

With his head relaxed against the chair, Roy smiled up at the sky. But rather than answer Pat's question, he closed his eyes and began to snore loud enough to wake the dead.

Chapter 10

Hidden behind the longest curtains on this side of heaven, B.J. was within perfect earshot of the cop's conversation with the guy named Roy—and he was not impressed with Roy. He had a highfalutin attitude that suggested that he was above the law. Had he come down from his high horse and told the officer where to find Woody, B.J. would've left as quietly as he'd come. Instead, Roy had chosen to thumb his nose at the cop, bringing on his worst nightmare, a man who wasn't constrained by legal rigmarole. When the cop was gone, B.J. flexed his fingers in preparation for a throwdown. He knew that no one was there except him and Roy, so there would be no witnesses and no one to stop him from beating Roy to a pulp.

As his quarry slept like a log, B.J. stood over him, assessing his scrawny appearance. He had probably never done a hard day's work in his life, and for that, he should be grateful. But if he was Woody's brotherly friend as he'd said, then Roy was probably scum like his friend. And he deserved to be thumped.

To set the tone for their conversation, he decided to wake up Roy by placing his palm over Roy's big mouth to stop the airflow. But before he could, someone called out from inside the house. Surprised, B.J. sprinted to a cabana and ducked down.

In defiance of the Sheriff's orders, Fern had parked around the corner from Roy's home and waited for Pat to leave. She'd made up her mind to talk to Roy regardless of how Pat felt about it. Her butt was in a sling, and three conniving men—Roy, Woody, and Calvin—had conspired to put it there, using her marital hellhole to cover their tracks. The pieces were starting to fit together—Woody's disappearance, the fake drugs, B.J. She didn't understand why Woody was the only one in hiding, but that was a question for another day. The more pressing matter was the knife that he'd plunged into her back. There were some things that a man just shouldn't do, like set up the mother of his children to go to prison on false charges. Woody had always had a yellow streak, but he'd gone way too far this time.

As soon as she saw the Sheriff leave, she drove back to Roy's house and rang the doorbell. After waiting a suitable amount of time, she opened the door and poked her head inside.

"Hello?" There was no response. "Hello?" She stepped inside. "Roy? It's Fern. I need to talk to you." Still, no one answered. She walked aimlessly around the rooms in search of any of the residents. It had been many years since she'd last been here, and she liked the changes that Mrs. Gerritson had made. The brown wooden walls that Fern remembered were now painted bright colors that reflected Maggie's cheerful personality. She had also replaced the carpet with wall-to-wall hardwood flooring. Fern couldn't imagine what the cost must've been. Redecorating a house would be a frivolous expense for her. And it was reminders like this that triggered her resentment for Woody, a shameless moocher, but she set aside her frustration, as his whereabouts had become a higher priority.

She eventually reached the sliding doors that led to the backyard, where she could hear the rumble of someone's obnoxious snoring. Roy was out cold with his mouth wide open, and she was tempted to drop a spider into it. But no bug deserved such a horrible death, so she settled for using her purse to strike him good and hard.

"Hey!" He was jolted awake and clutched his chest as though expecting to find a wound. "What the hell!" He sat up and met Fern's angry gaze. "Did you just hit me?"

"No." He stank of alcohol, and there was a tall, empty glass beside him. "Are you drunk?"

"No, I'm not drunk." His words were slurred, but he seemed to have a grasp on reality. "I had a little to drink."

"Sure you did. Enough to fill an abyss."

"How did you get here? You're trespassing!"

"I want to know about the pills that you boys have been selling."

"What pills? I don't know what you're talking about."

"Stop lying! The Sheriff found pills under my bed, and I know that you, Woody, and Calvin were up to something. Now you're trying to worm your way out of trouble by telling everyone that I killed Woody, but it's not going to work because I'm onto you, all of you. And pretty soon, everybody in town is gonna know what I know."

"Everybody already knows that you, Jasmine, and your crazy father—"

"I know that the pills were made from Tylenol. And I know that Woody's alive because people have seen him. He's hiding from B.J."

"Well, Miss Brainiac, you've just solved the riddle. All we need to do is find B.J., and then Woody will magically reappear. There's just one big problem—there is no B.J."

"Then who came to my house looking for Woody? Huh? Tell me that, because it sure wasn't Santa Claus. The fact that you can look me in the eyes and lie through your teeth makes me sick. We both know that Woody wants B.J. to think he's dead."

"The only thing I know is that you're delusional. You've lost your mind."

"Where is Woody hiding, Roy?"

"You know better than I do where he is. Why don't you just own up to what you've done and tell the Sheriff where you buried the body?"

"You are lower than a snake's belly," Fern seethed.

"Get out of here before I call the Sheriff to report you for trespassing!"

"You won't get away with this. You have my word."

"That sounds a lot like your last words to Woody." He reached for a cell phone. "I'm sure the Sheriff would like to know that your handiwork isn't finished. Under the circumstances, he might think that I need police protection."

"Go to hell!"

As he dialed a phone number, Fern rushed from the house and slammed the door, furious with Roy's smugness. He was sticking to his story, and she was pulling her hair out. She wouldn't be waiting for Consuela to call her. They needed to talk now because Fern could feel the walls closing in on her.

While the canopy had provided good cover, its location had prevented B.J. from hearing Roy's and Fern's conversation. He could see that they were annoyed with each other, but that was it, not that it mattered. He already knew what he needed to know. Roy possessed the information that B.J. wanted, and B.J. was willing to break his arms and legs to get it.

After Fern left, B.J. emerged from behind the canopy and strode toward Roy, who was distracted with his phone. He didn't look up until B.J.'s body blocked the sun—and by then, it was too late for him to run.

"Who the hell are you?"

B.J. knocked Roy's phone from his hands while giving him a death stare. "I'm B.J."

While some said that there was no honor among thieves, Pat could personally attest that the code of silence among them was alive and well. After leaving Roy's house with nothing gained for a second time, Pat thought carefully about how best to pry someone's mouth open. So far he'd been met with hardcore resistance in every discussion conducted on someone else's turf. He needed to mix things up and get people on his, starting with Shasta. To most, the police station was a green goblin that nobody wanted to see. And Shasta had revealed herself as one such person last year when he'd brought her in with a threat of booking her. If he got her back to the station, he might finally shake some fruit from the tree.

"Papa Bear, it's the Junkyard Dog. Come back." Chip was trying to reach him on the CB. A diehard wrestling fan, he had lobbied for the handle Junkyard Dog, one of his all-time favorite pros.

"Papa Bear here, J.D. What's your 20?"

"I'm at the Lekker River, and reporting an all clear." In this case, "all clear" meant that Woody's body was nowhere in sight. Nor was there any evidence of suspicious activities. Pat had not expected a different outcome.

"10-4, J.D. I have another assignment for you. Go pick up our commercial company and take her to the bear cave as soon as you get her."

"A 10-38, sir?" He needed to know if a warrant for Shasta's arrest had been issued.

"No, just another talk about our 6-0-1. Do you have her 10-85?"

"That's a 10-4, Papa Bear. Rolling. Over and out."

While Chip carried out his orders to collect Shasta, Pat drove to Mercury Street, where drugs were treated like one of the five food groups. He and Deputy Lester Davis were going to question the residents, taking another stab at a population that had already told Lester where he could stick his questions about Woody. The day was young, and Pat tried to hold out hope that it could still be a good one—and his hopes weren't entirely unfounded. Odell's keen nose for evidence had come through, finding white dog fur and a mysterious thumbprint in Cricket's car. Either or both could be crucial to breaking the case, and Pat had immediately warned his whole team to keep a lid on Odell's report. He was sure that the dog fur was linked to Shasta's poodle even though they couldn't justify spending money to confirm it. This was his opportunity to scare her into thinking that she was going down for killing Woody. When they spoke, he would say that the fur proved that Woody had stolen the dog, after which she'd made him pay with his life. Maybe to save herself, she would roll over and tell him where to find Woody, validating all the sightings that Pat was hearing about. Although he couldn't think of any reason for her to be in cahoots with Woody, that didn't mean anything.

Regardless of how things went with Shasta, he was consoled by the thumbprint, which couldn't lie or deny facts. Odell had found it on the rearview mirror, and now they needed to know who it belonged to. No matches came up in the state or federal databases, but preliminary analysis pointed to a male—a tall one who'd pushed the driver's seat back far enough to accommodate legs that were too long to be attached to Woody, Fern, or Cricket. It seemed that this male was the last person who had driven the car and seen Woody, a speculation that was just that. Pat would prefer to have a lot more to go on, but something was better than nothing.

On spotting Lester, Pat pulled up alongside him to wave before parking. As the two most seasoned members of the force, they enjoyed an easygoing bond and had similar hobbies like fishing. Together, they walked around the neighborhood and spoke to anyone who was willing, which wasn't many. As usual, most residents treated them like pariahs. Those who did talk unanimously stated that they hadn't seen Woody—and frankly, Pat believed them.

Discouraged, they walked back to Pat's car. "Sorry, boss, that we didn't get anything worth having. I warned you not to get your hopes up. This crowd only cares about getting their next fix."

"I know, but I had to try."

Lester leaned against the car. "I honestly don't think that Woody came to this neighborhood."

"I don't think so either, but he's gotten into something somewhere that went south. The pills under his bed, Cricket's car being abandoned at the warehouse...I don't know what's going on, but it's not good."

"Do you still think that Fern is a viable suspect?"

"Not really. You wanna know the truth? I think that I have several potential suspects and no suspects at all. It's the damndest thing. I wish I knew who left that thumbprint. If I could find that person, I could solve this case."

"Boss, it's possible that Woody left of his own volition. Maybe he pushed the wrong person too far and had to run for it."

"I've thought about that. But what about Cricket's car being left at the warehouse?"

"Maybe one of his chums helped him to vanish and then took the car to the warehouse. Calvin is over six feet, isn't he? He fits Odell's estimate of the driver's height."

"But that's not Calvin's thumbprint on the rearview mirror. We already checked."

"He voluntarily provided his fingerprints?"

"No." Pat sheepishly looked over his shoulder to ensure that no one was around to overhear him. "I asked Miguel to watch his garage this morning and bring back any cups or cans that Calvin threw away."

"That was slick." Lester laughed.

"His juvie records were expunged and I wasn't going to get his prints if I asked. You know Calvin."

"Yeah, but who says that the thumbprint belongs to whoever left the car? It could've been there for weeks. Cricket is a popular girl with a lot of friends."

"We're almost certain that it's a male thumbprint."

"Does she have a boyfriend?"

"That's a good question that I'll have to ask." Pat remembered the condoms he'd found in Cricket's bedroom. He hadn't wanted to open that can of worms, but he might not have a choice. "Dammit, this thing is one big mess."

"That, my friend, is the understatement of the year."

Pat's eyes fell behind Lester, who turned to see what had lured his attention. They watched as a teenage ne'er-do-well nicknamed Goose approached them. Wearing checkered boxers and jeans that were belted around his thighs, he wasn't the most promising informant. But Pat was long-past desperate and willing to give almost anyone the benefit of the doubt.

"What do you think he wants?" Pat dared to hope that Goose was going to give the code of silence a good kick in the teeth.

"I guess we'll find out. I don't trust him, though. He's turned out several young girls, and I've been busting my ass to get enough proof to take him off the streets."

"His file is a mile high, but if he's got information that helps my case, I'm taking it." Pat took a couple of steps forward to stand side by side with Lester.

"Yo! Mr. Sheriff." Goose was talking before he was within arm's length. "I heard that you're lookin' for Woody Walker."

"That's right. You know him?"

"Yeah, I know him. I've seen him a few times."

"Where did you see him?"

Goose was now close enough for Pat to touch him. "Before I tell you that, you hafta agree to my terms."

"And what might those be?" Pat crossed his arms.

"Nothin much. I just want twenty bucks."

"I don't have twenty bucks. But I do have a set of handcuffs that I can use to arrest you for attempting to extort an officer."

"Chill out, sir. Chill out. Okay, if you don't have twenty dollars, I'll offer you a basement bargain. I'll tell you what I know for the unbeatable price of ten dollars."

"Ten dollars? Why, I oughta—"

"Relax, boss. I'll handle this." Lester warily eyeballed Goose. "Why don't you tell us what you know, and we'll give you ten dollars if it's useful?"

"Come on, sir! I wasn't born yesterday. Pay me up front, or I'll just keep what I know to myself." He looked at Pat again. "We got a deal?"

"Don't do it, boss. He's pulling your leg."

"If you want to find Woody, then you'll pay me." Goose smiled, revealing gold-capped front teeth.

"Don't do it, Pat. He'd sell his own grandmother before helping us."

Against Lester's objections, Pat reached for his wallet. "All right, Goose, I'll give you the money. But you'd better have good information, or I'm going to arrest you here and now."

"You won't regret it, Sheriff."

Goose held out his palm, and Pat placed a crisp ten-dollar bill in it. Goose then held the bill up to his nose and smelled it.

"I've met my end of the bargain. Now it's your turn."

"I'm a man of my word." Goose paused to smile and wink at Lester. Then he took off running down the street. Lester immediately gave chase, but Pat already knew that the pursuit was hopeless. Two old men didn't stand a chance of catching a teenager, not even on their best day.

As Pat watched Goose round a corner, his phone vibrated in his shirt pocket. "Yeah, Dottie, what's up?"

"Sheriff, a call just came in from Memorial Hospital. Roy Gerritson was found unconscious at home. They're saying that he was beat up real bad."

"By who?"

"They don't know. He was alone when his mother found him."

"All right. I'm on my way." Pat sprinted to his car and sped off with his sirens blaring.

Chapter 11

Being of royal birth in his own mind, Roy had been too dense to recognize the colossal problem standing over him. Rather than showing due respect to B.J., he'd launched into a litany of insults while trying to call the cops. Both actions had been foolish, and B.J. had let his fists do the talking until a few of Roy's bones and his spirit were broken. At the sight of his own blood spurting into his hands, Roy had bawled like a newborn baby. Then he'd coughed up the name of a hotel in Mexico before crumpling to the ground in a mangled heap. By the time B.J. left him, he was in no condition to call anyone.

Putting Roy in his place had given B.J. immense gratification. And doing the same to Woody would feel even better. Soon B.J.'s wish would be granted because he now knew where to find Woody. According to Roy, Woody had used a forged passport and a fake name to cross the border. There, he was supposed to keep his head down until the coast was clear—meaning, until B.J. had stopped looking for him. His buddies had even started rumors that Woody was dead, thinking that this would derail B.J.'s resolve to find him. The more he heard, the more he realized that he was dealing with guys who slept with smiles on their faces after wreaking havoc on innocent people. And from B.J.'s perspective, a man with no principles wasn't worth one damned thing.

Having no current passport with him, B.J. gave the border agent a generous fifty-dollar tip to let him pass. He winced while forking over the cash. It was like flushing money down the toilet, but he'd come too far to turn back. Steam spewed from his ears as he reached the hotel and gave the front desk clerk Woody's fake name, Johnny Cash. While she checked the computer, he looked around the lobby. The place was decent, maybe a little run-down, but clean. Woody wouldn't be suffering here, but his stay was going to be cut short—or so B.J. thought. Unfortunately, it turned out that no one named Johnny Cash had ever checked in. Nor had anyone named Woody Walker. Enraged at Roy's deception, B.J. clinched his fists while charging back to his truck. "That low-down, lying maggot!" He struck his steering wheel before starting the truck and speeding back across the border, back to Fern's house, where he would have no choice but to unleash the devil inside him.

When Pat reached the hospital, he rushed straight to Roy's room, where he was startled at the sight that greeted him. The guy was in bad shape, bandaged almost entirely from head to toe. Both of his parents were sitting near the bed, and Maggie was clutching Roy's hand as if it were her very heart.

"Sheriff." A nurse approached him. "We've given him a sedative. He'll be asleep for a good while."

"Is he going to make a full recovery?"

"The doctor thinks so, but he's got a long road ahead. Three of his ribs and his nose are broken as well as his left arm. We're also treating internal bleeding."

Pat shook his head solemnly and turned to Maggie and Roy Sr. as the nurse left the room. Maggie had obviously been crying. "I'm truly sorry that this has happened." What he didn't say was that Roy had very likely earned his whipping.

"Thank you for coming, Sheriff." Maggie sniffled. "We're just in shock. We don't know why—" Sobs spilled from her as Roy Sr. held her.

"What she's trying to say is that we don't know who would want to hurt our boy. He was barely conscious when Maggie found him."

"Did he say anything to either of you before he was sedated? Did he say who'd done this to him?"

"He just kept saying 'Fern,' 'Fern,' 'Fern,'" Maggie sputtered. "But Fern couldn't've done this. I mean, look at him. He's black and blue in every place we can see."

"We were thinking that somebody must've come over to rob the house and worked him over to shut him up. That's the only thing that makes any sense."

"Did you notice anything missing in the house?"

"I didn't look." Maggie's teary eyes fell back on her son's swollen face. "I don't care if anything was stolen. All I care about is my son getting back on his feet."

"I understand that, and I'm deeply sorry. But we will need to know if anything is missing from the house. It'll help with our investigation."

"Well, your investigation will have to wait because I'm not leaving my son."

"Pat, I'll be at home later this evening to pick up some things that we'll need while we're at the hospital." Roy Sr. seemed to be more in control of his emotions. "If anything was taken, I'll let you know."

"That would be greatly appreciated." Pat again looked at Roy, who had received a brutal bashing. He agreed with Maggie that Fern couldn't possibly be the perpetrator. Nor could anyone else who was on his short list of suspects. But there was no doubt that someone with a personal vendetta had acted on it. When Roy woke up, maybe he would finally quit all the lies.

In the meantime, there was nothing here for Pat to do. "Ellie and I will pray for Roy's swift recovery."

"That's mighty kind of you. We'll take all the prayers that we can get." Maggie used a Kleenex to dab at her eyes as Pat left them.

His mind was completely scrambled as he searched for an explanation for Roy's thrashing. While Roy Sr. suspected burglary, Pat felt that Woody was somehow connected. But whether that connection was through Fern, the phony drugs, or something else remained a mystery.

"I heard that the Sheriff's tipline is blowing up with calls from people who claim to have seen Woody, but without any video, it's all hearsay." In a rare appearance at the diner, Jasmine had come by after getting off of work to offer support to Fern. Seated at the bar, she drank Coca-Cola while Fern watched the door. The evening crowd hadn't yet trickled in, but the frenzy over the news story about Woody had finally blown over. "Sure would be nice if more houses and business establishments had cameras."

"Do you think that anyone has actually seen him?"

"Yeah, I do. But I don't know if they're right about when they've seen him. That's the problem."

"Fern," Deedee bellowed from the back. "You've got a call."

Fern rolled her eyes at Jasmine. "People keep calling with tips about Woody. It's like working at crazytown."

"Tell them to call the Sheriff before they cost you your job."

"I don't want to do that because I don't trust the Sheriff." Fern threw a dish towel over her shoulder. "I'll be right back." She walked to the phone. "This is Fern."

"Hi, Fern. It's Consuela."

"I hope you're calling with good news."

"I wish I were, but I'm not. I just found out that Woody's friend Roy is in the hospital. Somebody knocked him into the middle of next week. Broken bones, busted nose, the whole nine."

Fern's jaw hit the floor. "Who would want to do that?"

"Nobody knows, but his mother says that Roy was saying your name when she found him."

"I don't know why that would be. Whatever happened, I don't have anything to do with it. Is he going to live?"

"He'll recover. And for the record, nobody thinks that you harmed Roy. The injuries are far too catastrophic for any woman to have caused them. I was wondering if you think that B.J. might've done this to him. My people haven't found him yet, but if he's as big as you say he is, maybe he went after Roy to get to Woody."

"Oh...maybe." She turned around so she could again watch the door. "If he can't find Woody, he might—" She gulped. "He might go after anyone who knows him. He might be on a rampage."

"Now, Fern, I don't want you to worry. If he's still in town, we'll find him. I'm looking for him, and so is the Sheriff."

"Pat ain't looking for him. Pat thinks I made him up to turn his gun in a different direction."

"He might think that, but he still has to investigate. That's his job. I've already confirmed that they're trying to find B.J., but he's not staying at any hotels. It's possible he already left town. We just don't know."

Fern remained silent, her thoughts having turned to her children.

"Are you still there?"

"Yeah, I'm here, but my children are at home alone, and he knows where we live. I can't afford to leave this godforsaken job, but I can't stay here if they're in danger."

"Hold your horses. Nothing's going to happen to them. If B.J. were going to hurt them, he already would've done it. And like I said, we don't know who has it in for Roy or why. He could've just been at home at the wrong time. His parents think that someone attempted to rob the place."

"But you think it was B.J."

"I have my suspicions, yes. But no one has seen B.J. except you, so it's hard to say if my instincts are right."

Fern's defenses surged. "Do you agree with the Sheriff that I made him up?"

"Of course not. I'm on your side. And if he's still in Luna, I'll find him. I've got to know whatever he knows about Woody. It could be crucial to building our case against the ideas floating around in Pat's head."

"Okay." Fern released a long breath. "I've gotta get back to work. There's customers coming in."

"Before you go, I need to tell you one more thing. The Sheriff needs your and Cricket's fingerprints."

"For what?"

"Only so they can accurately identify any strange prints lifted from Cricket's car."

"Are you sure that's the only reason?"

"Yes. He's asking if you'll go by the station tomorrow at a time that works best for you and Cricket. And while you're there, you can get her car back."

"I think it's an ambush. He wants to get me there so he can arrest me."

"He has no reason to do that. He just wants your prints and to know whether anyone besides family members has driven the car. That's it."

"Oh, all right," she grumbled. "I'm trusting you. The best time for us to go will be around two. I'll have to get Cricket out of school early."

"Then two it is, and I'll meet you at the front door."

"Okay, I'll see you tomorrow." Unsettled by the Sheriff's request, Fern's heart was in her mouth as she rushed to obtain her customers' orders. As soon as they were taken care of, she shared all that Consuela had said with Jasmine.

"It's about time somebody kicked Roy's ass. I don't feel sorry for him."

"I know. Same here. I only care about me and my family."

"Me, too. But this B.J. guy…he's an enigma. I'd give a million bucks to know what Woody did to piss him off. You got a gun at the house in case he comes back?"

"No! And I don't want one. Anyway, Consuela doesn't think that we're in danger. His business is with Woody."

"Hmph. Woody and Roy, it seems. Probably Calvin, too. We don't often see people like B.J. around Luna, though, so I think I should bring you one of my guns just to be safe."

"I said no guns, and I mean it. I don't want them in my house around my children."

Jasmine merely sipped from her glass before standing up. "Fine, have it your way. You and Consuela seem to have things under control." She pecked Fern's cheek and headed for the exit. "If you change your mind about the gun, call me."

Chapter 12

Pat had always enjoyed fishing. He felt that it required skills that were similar to those that he used every day on the job. In order to catch a big fish, he had to have the right bait and hold it steady for as long as it took for the fish to bite. This exercise demanded a great deal of patience and submission to an unpredictable outcome. Sometimes the fish never bit, regardless of how well he'd prepared or how long he waited. Sometimes he caught a basketful and reveled in his good fortune. Either way, he never went home disappointed. Instead, he always felt refreshed, as though the water had given him something to restore his soul even if it hadn't filled his stomach. But this was where the similarities between fishing and his job parted ways. He could never be satisfied with fishing for missing people or lawbreakers and reeling in the line without a catch. Doing so meant that someone's family was being denied closure or justice, neither of which was acceptable. Nevertheless, this seemed to be the direction that Woody's case was going. And Pat was gnashing his teeth as he strolled into the station, where Shasta waited to be questioned. After making a pit stop, he swung by Dottie's desk for any important updates, particularly about Shasta's behavior while she'd sat alone in the interview room. Guilty suspects often paced, made frantic phone calls, or cried. And Pat had his fingers crossed that Shasta had exhibited at least one such telltale sign.

"How's she been doing in there? Does she seem nervous or upset?"

"Nope. She asked for a bag of Funyuns and a bottle of water. Haven't heard a peep out of her since."

"Huh. That's not what I wanted to hear." He sighed. "What else you got?"

"The judge just approved the warrant for Fern's and Hiram's cell phone records. We won't get 'em faster than grass grows, though."

"I know. Bureaucracy at its finest. It's starting to feel like nothing but a check in the box anyway. With Roy all beat up, my money is on him, Woody, and Calvin having gotten into something that boomeranged on them."

"Sheriff Dupree, I'd like to have a word with you."

Pat looked in the direction of the voice and saw Jasmine coming toward him. "Well, this is a surprise. Are you sure you want to talk to me without a lawyer?"

"I don't need a lawyer." Jasmine haughtily eyed him. "I haven't done anything that warrants lawyering."

"Neither have your sister or father, according to them. But they've hired Consuela."

"You can blame yourself for that. Can we talk in private?"

Pat thought about Shasta for a split second but then resignedly nodded and led her to his office. "So, to what do I owe the pleasure of your visit?" He kicked back in his chair.

"I want to know what you're doing to find the man named B.J., whose been looking for Woody."

"Oh, well, we're doing the best we can, but I don't have a lot of resources to find phantoms."

"He's not a phantom. I think he's the one who whupped Roy. Did that occur to you?"

"I've heard the theory; however, I can't be expected to arrest thin air."

"See, I knew it. You've got your blinders on, Pat. And your thickheaded thinking is not helping my sister. For all we know, B.J. is coming for her next."

Pat placed a hand under his jaw for a brief moment. Jasmine was in his territory, and he needed to take advantage of this stroke of luck. "You're right. Why don't you have a seat and get comfortable? I want to know everything you can tell me about B.J."

"I know as much as you do. And don't try that cop crap with me because I'm not as dumb as most of the people who come through here. I want you to get your ass in gear and find B.J. before he beats someone else to the ground."

"How can you be so sure that B.J. assaulted Roy? Have you seen him?"

"I don't need to see him. I believe Fern."

"Would you also believe that Fern could've been mad enough at Woody to hire B.J. to kill him?"

Jasmine laughed sardonically. "And pay him with what? Her good looks?"

"I don't know. You tell me. Is there an insurance policy on Woody?"

"Good lord. You really are a piece of work, you know that?"

"Or maybe you're the one who hired B.J., and now you want to muddy the waters of my investigation to stop me from arresting Fern. Is that it?" Pat was just throwing out random thoughts to see how she reacted. So far, she was not a fish who'd taken the bait.

"First you said he's a phantom. Now you say he's a hitman. Your head is stuck so far up your ass that you could lick your nostrils clean."

"Is that right? Well, tell me this—where were you on the night that Woody went missing? Since you don't need a lawyer, you shouldn't mind telling me."

"I was at work, and you can check the logs on my computer to prove it."

"Working at nine o'clock at night? Isn't that a little late?"

"It's what I do, Sheriff. And it's becoming painfully obvious that I work a lot harder than you do." She flung the door open and angrily stomped out, leaving Pat with a new, intriguing thought. On his way to Shasta, he passed by Dottie and asked, "How tall is B.J. based on Fern's description?"

"I don't recall exactly. Over six feet." She looked for the notes.

"I wonder if he's the fella who drove Cricket's car to the warehouse. That is, assuming that he exists."

"But isn't he supposedly looking for Woody?"

"That's what Fern says, but I don't know if it's true. Do me a favor and put out an APB for anyone matching B.J.'s description in Luna. If he's flesh and blood, I want him found."

Both rankled and worn out, B.J. drove past Fern's house without stopping. Her car wasn't in the driveway, and given the late hour, he was fairly certain that she wouldn't be back until tomorrow morning. From what he'd seen while watching the house, she worked as a waitress at night. And with observant neighbors around, it wasn't in his best interest to stake out her house in plain view again. So he'd instead get a room where he could have a hot bath, hot food, and a warm bed. The change would do him good since sleeping in his truck had started to give him back pains, reminding him that he was no spring chicken. He was already looking forward to stretching out on a mattress.

Soon after checking into a cheap hotel, he was standing in the shower as steaming water washed away all the grime that had accumulated on his skin and in his hair. The smell of the soap made him feel human again, and for a moment, he questioned whether a thousand dollars was really worth all the trouble that he'd gone to. But just as quickly as the thought crossed his mind, it vanished. He knew that he could never stand by and let someone take advantage of him as he'd seen his feckless family members do to people. Swindlers, cheapskates, and vagrants weren't separated by much, and it was the responsibility of those they targeted to put them in their place. Tomorrow, he would do just that and conclude his affairs in Luna.

Pat entered the interview room and found Shasta engaged with something on her cell phone as if she had no cares in the world. On this occasion, her purple braids were hanging free and falling forward around her face. Her nails were painted red and were so long that they brought witch claws to mind.

"Thank you for waiting, Shasta." He closed the door and sat across the table from her.

"I didn't think I had a choice." She tucked her braids behind her ears, one of those niggling indications that he would soon be awash in her lies.

"I need to follow up on the conversation we had a couple of days ago. You told me that Woody spent the night at your apartment several times."

"That's right."

"Did he sleep in your bed, on your couch, or what?"

"He slept with me." She smiled. "I mean, he slept in my bed, and that was all he did."

"What's your dog's name?"

"Pudding. Why?"

"You seem to love her very much."

"I sure do. She's my precious little baby."

"Does she sleep in your bed?"

"Of course."

"Even when Woody was sleeping over?"

"Yeah, but what does that have to do with anything?"

"Did Woody ever take Pudding with him when he left your apartment?"

"Absolutely not. Pudding stays with me at all times."

"That's interesting because a few people have told me that Woody did, in fact, take Pudding and he sold her without your permission. Is that true?"

"Hell to the no! He'd never be so stupid."

"What would happen if he did it? What would you do if he took Pudding away from you?"

"I'd probably cut his throat. But since that didn't happen, I don't understand why you're asking me these questions. Did you actually bring me here to talk about my dog?" She looked incredulous.

"Has Pudding ever been in Woody's car?"

"For what?"

Pat shrugged innocently. "Maybe he dropped her off at the groomer for you."

"I just said that Pudding doesn't go anywhere without me." She crossed her legs and began to shake the one on top.

"Have you ever been in Woody's car?"

"I don't like these questions. Are you accusing me of something that I need to get a lawyer for?"

Pat groaned inwardly at the mention of a lawyer. "I'm not accusing you of anything, Shasta. I'm just asking questions that shouldn't be a problem if you're being straight with me."

"I've told you the truth, but you don't seem to believe it. And I'm not saying anything else unless my attorney is present.

You can't hold my face under the water like you did the last time I was here. I know my rights now."

Her newfound knowledge had shut him down. By law, he couldn't ask her anything else without her attorney in the room. Pat wanted to kick the table, but he restrained himself.

"Am I under arrest, or am I free to go?"

"You can go."

"Is Chip going to take me back home?"

"Yeah, let's go get him." He escorted her down the hall and then skulked back to his office, where he could now freely release his frustration with a swift kick at his desk. He'd gone into the interview with minimal expectations, but that didn't make him feel any better about the results—or the lack thereof. When it came down to it, he had no evidence that Woody's disappearance was the result of a crime. He had no body, no blood, no crime scene, no weapons, nothing. What he did have was a fool who could've gone into hiding as a consequence of his own bad behavior. And now that fool had Pat running a fool's errand—and he was getting damned tired of it. He stewed in his frustration until his eyes fell on the doorway. To his surprise, Lester was standing there with Goose in handcuffs.

"Look who I found when I was patrolling Mercury Street."

"Well, I'll be." Pat got to his feet and walked over to stand in front of Goose, who was wearing his bravest face. "Justice has a long arm, Goose. You got my ten dollars?"

"No, sir. I used the money to buy food for my grandmother. Her social security check isn't enough for her to live on."

"That's a really sad story. I'll bet you use it all the time. Too bad for you that I know your grandmother, and I know that she has enough money to take cruises every year."

"She saves money for the cruises instead of buying food."

"She doesn't look like she's missed any meals as far as I can see. What do you think, Lester? Is Mrs. Dunwoody going hungry?"

"Not by a longshot. I see her at church every Sunday, and she's as fit as a fiddle."

"You hear that, Goose? She's as fit as a fiddle. So I'll ask you again. Where is my money?"

"I don't have it, sir."

"All right. Lester, book him for theft and lock him up."

"But, sir! I'm only sixteen. I'm still a minor."

"You'll be taken to the juvie hall as soon as they can come get you. When you're older and wiser, you'll thank me."

"But, sir—"

"Get him outta here, Lester."

"My pleasure."

Pat grinned with satisfaction as Lester dragged Goose away.

Chapter 13

Fern was in the dumps about having to work a double shift, but her monthly budget had been put through the ringer by all the hours she'd lately missed on the job. Making this month's tally come together was going to require her most acrobatic balancing act. As if squeezing every nickel wasn't hard enough, now she had to squeeze every penny.

As she worked that morning, she watched the clock, having committed to being at the police station with Cricket by two. While there, they would retrieve Cricket's car, after which Fern would return to work for her normal shift. The next twenty-four hours were going to be rough, and she would have to muster everything she was made of to stay awake. But she took heart from the community's support, an unexpected silver lining, as everyone did what they could to ease her burdens. Customers' tips had substantially increased, and their conversations were filled with concern for her welfare. Even Bernie had offered her a loan that she could pay back whenever she had the money, but she had graciously refused out of pride.

Invisible arms had been wrapped around her, holding her up for as long as she needed them. And the collective kindness had made her feel like the world hadn't turned against her after all. There was a light at the end of the tunnel.

Having a case of sore feet, Fern took a break and tottered to the back to rub them. The bunions were red and inflamed, but there was nothing she could do about it. She was wiggling her toes when Jared came in.

"Thank God it's Friday. I'm taking the weekend off and hitting the beach."

"Good for you. I'll be picking up another shift." She grimaced as she shoved her feet back into her shoes. "I've still got some time to make up before I can take a day to rest. And when I do, I'm going to sleep like there's no tomorrow."

"As well you should. And maybe now you can start living it up a little. You've shed a lot of extra pounds now that Woody is off of your back."

"That would be premature, dontcha think? He ain't dead. He's just missing."

"Until I see him with my own eyes, I won't know what he is. As far as I'm concerned, you're a free woman. You can kick up your heels and have some fun."

Fern cackled at the thought. "If only it were that easy. But like my daddy says, Woody is a cockroach and he'll be back. I think he's just biding his time until B.J. leaves town."

"Nobody's seen any strangers named B.J. Maybe he already left."

"I doubt it, especially now that somebody has put a hurting on Roy."

Jared shook his head and tutted. "Have you heard the latest rumors about what people think happened to Woody?"

"I hear something new every day. Why? What've you heard?"

"That he was watching YouTube videos about mind control so he could learn how to hypnotize people into giving him their money. But he accidently got hypnotized by one of the videos, and now his mind is wiped clean. They say that he's wandering around, probably lost in the woods somewhere, and sucking everything dry like a chupacabra."

"Who in their right mind could think such a thing?"

"Lionel said that his daughter heard it at the beauty shop."

"Well, it's nothing but gibberish, Jared. And you oughta know it because the only videos that Woody likes are games." She stood up and straightened her uniform, again wincing at the pain in her feet. "When I married him, I had a pretty high opinion of myself, but living by the skin of our teeth brought me back down to earth real fast. I realized that I'd made a big mistake, but I was too young and dumb to undo it. So I held on with a hope that things might one day get easy. And for a while, Woody and I were all right. I wasn't living a dream, but I couldn't complain. Not really. But everything went to hell in a handbasket when he quit his job and refused to get another one. It's like he changed into somebody who I don't know anymore—somebody I don't want to know. Something in him got broken, and I can't fix it."

"He's a grown man, Fern, and it's not your responsibility to fix him."

"I know, but—" She sighed. "You put twenty years into a relationship, and you don't want to see all of that go down the drain, especially when you've got kids. But I've learned my lesson from all of this. I won't be carrying him on my back anymore. Whenever he decides to come home, he'll have divorce papers waiting for him to sign."

Although B.J. had gotten the best sleep that he'd had since coming to Luna, the hotel mattress had only worsened his back pain. When he'd rolled over in the wee hours, he'd felt a twinge that had told him that bending down was going to be a problem for the rest of the day. But this inconvenience would not deter him. As long as he could walk, he would finish what he'd come to do.

After checking out of the hotel, he took a few moments to find a comfortable sitting position in his truck, one that minimized the jolts of pain that were zinging up and down his spine. Riding on bumpy roads would be out of the question, but keeling over didn't loom on his near horizon.

Upon reaching Fern's house, he was stunned that her car still wasn't parked in the driveway. But he saw the kids leaving for school, which set him at ease. She had not completely abandoned the place as Woody had. She would return at some point. In the meantime, he'd address his back pain, which was amping up more aggressively than he'd expected. In dire need of relief, B.J. went in search of the nearest drug store and the strongest remedy that he could buy without a prescription.

Now that the news of Woody's disappearance had circulated around town, the events that may have led to his departure had gotten even fuzzier. Folks from every corner had barraged Pat's staff with stories about Woody's clandestine schemes to swindle residents out of their money. And he hadn't been alone, as nearly every tale included his two brothers from different mothers. Through these testimonials, Pat also discovered that he'd been cut out of the grapevine for some time, hindering him from hearing about dastardly deeds that were happening right under his nose. If any of the accounts were true, they spelled big trouble for Woody. No one knew better than Pat that some of the most straightlaced citizens wore two faces. And when wronged, the face that fancied an eye for an eye would show itself. In these situations, there were no loose lips telling anyone where the bodies were buried. And heading for the hills would've been Woody's smartest move.

As Pat strolled to his vehicle that morning, he pondered whether he should heed his instincts to bring Calvin into the station for questioning. In light of his past, Calvin was an especially hard nut to crack, and he would come prepared to say little or nothing if talking meant incriminating either himself or his comrades. Although Pat detested subjecting himself to pointless endeavors, he called Dottie to ask that Calvin be brought in. Surprisingly, she informed him that Roy was awake and talking, a welcome development that easily preempted Calvin. Pat had to get to Roy while the getting was good.

On entering the hospital, the smell of sickness assailed his nose, giving rise to heartrending memories of the day his sweet mother had passed. It had been some years back, but it remained the most difficult day of his life. He suppressed the images of her decrepit body, a task made easier upon reaching Roy's room and hearing Maggie tell her nitwitted son how much she loved him. At that moment, Pat would've liked to put his boot straight up Roy's backside, but he had to play his cards right in hopes that Roy might actually cooperate with him.

"It's good to see you up and talking, Roy." Pat entered the room as Maggie smiled in his direction, a huge shift from the frail woman he'd seen yesterday. "Mind if we have a talk?"

"He doesn't have a lot of energy, Sheriff," Maggie answered for him. "But I've already told him that he needs to tell you as much as he can."

Roy only looked at Pat, not seeming to want anything to do him.

"Go on, honey. It's okay to talk to the Sheriff. He only wants to help."

"You can't help because I don't know what happened." Roy's speech was impeded due to his jaw being heavily bandaged. "The only thing I remember is seeing Fern and then waking up in this bed."

"Why would Fern be at your house?"

"I don't know. You'll have to ask her. I just remember seeing her, and after that my lights went out."

"Uh-huh." Pat was instantly annoyed at Fern's mutinous disobedience, but that didn't necessarily implicate her. He would have to request a brief Q and A with her when she came to the station later that day. "Are you saying that Fern did this to you?"

"I'm saying that she's the last person I saw, Sheriff. And that's all I remember. My head hurts like someone took an ax and split it wide open. If I could remember who'd done this to me, I'd tell you, but I don't." A few stray tears rolled down his cheeks, and he turned his eyes upward to the ceiling.

"Shh, honey, it's okay." Maggie leaned over and hugged him as best she could without placing her weight against his body. "We understand, sweetheart. Believe me, we understand."

"I swear to God that I don't remember."

Pat was unmoved by Roy's emotional display. "Why do you think that nothing was taken from the house?" Roy Sr. had fulfilled his promise to alert Pat to any stolen valuables.

"How should I know?"

"Now, Pat," Maggie chimed in, "we told you that whoever did this probably didn't expect to find anyone at home when they came."

"That may be true, but it also implies that the intruder doesn't live in Luna. It's no secret that Roy has a DUI and stays at home most of the time." He turned his attention back to Roy, who had begun to rub his neck. "What can you tell me about a guy named B.J.?"

At this, Roy's body visibly stiffened, which didn't bode well for Pat's chances at getting an honest answer.

"Did you hear my question?"

"Yeah, I did, and the answer is nothing. I don't know anyone named B.J. Nobody whatsoever."

"Are you sure about that? Because it kinda looks like you do."

"No, I do not." Roy looked straight ahead as Maggie stroked his hair.

"Sheriff, if he says that he doesn't know him, then let him be. We've never heard of B.J. Is he the person who assaulted my son?"

"I don't know, and it'll be really hard to find out if Roy won't dish the dirt."

"Well, he's already said that he doesn't know who you're talking about, and I don't want him to get more upset than he already is. Maybe you should come back next week when he's feeling better. Maybe he'll remember something by then."

Judging by the way Roy was staring at the wall, he wouldn't be remembering anything anytime soon. And frankly, Pat wasn't too keen on trying to help a man who clearly didn't want to help himself. His head had been bashed in, and his reaction suggested that he'd deserved it. Pat was certain that Roy knew who B.J. was and why he'd taken Roy to the woodshed. But whatever scheme had brought on the attack had also clamped Roy's tongue, making Pat's way forward a brutally steep climb. He would have to try his luck with Calvin despite the dubious prospects. Once again, he called Dottie, and once again, she surprised him with a bulletin that was hot off the press.

"I was just about to call and tell you to go see Trixie at the Rosemont Hotel. She says that someone with the initials B.J. was at the hotel last night and he's bigger than the Green Giant."

Chapter 14

Finally, a stranger with the initials B.J. and a physical description that matched Fern's report had surfaced. Pat could look at it two different ways. Either B.J. had come to town to settle a score, as she'd said, or he'd come to do her bidding. Pat had seen it all while on the force, and he'd learned not to overlook any possibilities. The very one that seemed to be the most unlikely could turn out to be the right one. And B.J.'s mere existence renewed Pat's doubts about Fern's culpability.

Trixie hadn't known where B.J. had gone after leaving the hotel, but she'd noticed him holding his back as he'd walked to his vehicle. Logically, this infirmity cast doubt over Pat's new line of reasoning, but he still wrote down B.J.'s full name, the information about his vehicle, and the license plate. Then he radioed the station to have B.J.'s background checked so he would have a better idea of who he was dealing with. What came back was a stellar military record and no criminal history.

More importantly, B.J.'s fingerprints didn't match the one found on Cricket's rearview mirror.

"Damn!"

Every road had so far come to a dead end. Everything that seemed plausible was unprovable. And he could add all the rumors about Shasta to that pile, even though she had twitched like a flea-bitten dog during his interrogation yesterday. As long as he had no physical evidence, he was playing a guessing game. Flustered, he asked Dottie to line up the interview with Calvin and then he called Consuela to request a meeting with Fern.

Sightings of Woody continued to be shared with Fern, who was thrilled to bits with each one. There was no denying that Woody was alive and hiding somewhere, but until the Sheriff acknowledged what everyone else seemed to know, she had to stay on her p's and q's.

As she drove to pick up Cricket from school, she thought about how her children were feeling. They had to be hearing the same rumors as Fern, but they'd stopped talking much during breakfast. It was a tough situation, especially since she didn't share their despair for the same reasons. Her freedom had been deliberately jeopardized by a man who'd shown an utter disregard for her well-being. And though his blood ran through their veins, every bridge between him and Fern had been burned to the ground.

She watched Cricket drag herself outside to the car, her chin practically resting atop her chest. Woody had done this to her, that lousy piece of crap. What had he been thinking when he and his buddies had hatched their plan? The answer was obvious, of course. He hadn't been thinking, and that was the problem. That had been the problem for at least three years, and Fern needed to protect her children from such carelessness with their emotions. She would also have to explain that their father had disappeared, yes; however, he had made a bed that he must lie in as a consequence of his own choices. She didn't know when he'd be back, but she did know that he would show up when he was ready. Until then, they must not stop living their lives as if the world had stopped spinning. They must not shut themselves off in their grief. She would always be their backboard, and they could count on her for as long as there was breath in her body.

While en route to the police station, Fern heard from Consuela that Pat wanted to speak with her—and she nearly burst a blood vessel. She thoroughly dreaded the idea and considered making a U-turn. But Consuela assured her that she had nothing to fear. She would be stuck like glue to Fern's side, ready to nip Pat's antics in the bud. So despite her jitters, Fern had followed through and met Consuela at the front door with Cricket.

Up to this moment, the women had only spoken by phone, although Fern had seen photographs of Consuela posted on her employer's website. True to those photos, she was a beauty, as thin and comely as a ballerina. And her confidence radiated so brightly that she could've been a star. Standing next to her, Fern felt frumpy, like everything that she'd done in life except give birth to her children had been a mistake. At the same time, she realized that these types of self-critiques were pointless. She had much bigger fish to fry.

Consuela greeted them with hugs, saving her tighter embrace for Cricket, who remained sullen throughout. "Everything's going to be all right. When we go in, the Sheriff will have some questions for you and your mom. And I want you to be as honest as possible. We never know what little thing can help to bring your dad back home. Okay?"

Cricket wordlessly nodded as Consuela opened the door. Together, the three approached the front desk, at which point Dottie informed a deputy that Fern and Cricket had come to be fingerprinted. They swiftly completed the process and were escorted to an interview room, where Fern's teeth chattered as soon as she sat down.

This was the first time that she'd ever been in the same space that was typically reserved for criminals. Not only was the room uncomfortably cold, but Fern's nerves were racked. "Do we have to talk to Pat in here? Can't we go somewhere else?"

"Unfortunately, no. This is as good as it gets. Just relax. I'll handle Pat." Consuela was as cool as a cucumber, obviously in her element.

Within a few short minutes, Pat came into the room and took a seat with a steno pad and pen in hand. "Thank you all for coming. I really do appreciate you taking the time to help my investigation."

"We agreed to this meeting so that you'd stop playing pin the tail on the donkey with my clients. They have nothing to hide, and if this helps you to clear Fern, then we're all for it. So let's get down to business."

Pat and Consuela knew each other well, and he seemed to take her frosty demeanor in stride. "Fair enough. I'll start with you, Cricket. As you know, we located your car abandoned at an old warehouse. Can you tell me if anyone outside of your family has ever driven the car?"

"Not that I know of," she mumbled.

"Has anyone other than a family member had a reason to adjust the rearview mirror?"

"I...I don't know."

"You hesitated. Why's that?"

"Because I don't know if Daddy has ever let someone else drive the car when he's had it."

"I see. But you don't have any friends who've ever done something like use the rearview mirror to check their hair or makeup?"

"No, sir."

"No boyfriend?" At this question, Fern sat up alertly, thinking about the condoms that she hadn't yet mentioned to Cricket.

"No."

Fern was floored. "You're not seeing anyone at all?"

"No." She looked like the picture of innocence.

"What about Aden? You two seemed pretty cozy when I saw you at the football game."

"Aden? Seriously, Mama?" Cricket's bald disgust had brought her to life. "He's got pimples all over his face, and he's terrible at math. Why would I want to go out with somebody who can't even add numbers without a calculator?"

"Oh." Fern was chastened but not fully convinced. "Then why do you have—"

"Fern," Pat quickly interrupted, "if you don't mind, I'm the one asking the questions here."

"Agreed." Consuela glanced at Fern and Cricket. "Let's stick to the matters at hand."

Fern's eyes darted from Pat to Consuela before she acquiesced to their authority and slumped. Pat had undoubtedly seen where Fern's questions were going and intervened before she could hijack the discussion.

"All right." Pat restored his attention to Cricket. "I only have a couple more questions for you. Has Woody ever mentioned someone named B.J.?"

She shook her head as Fern's ears perked up once more.

"Are you sure about that?"

"Yes, I'm sure."

"How about the name Boone Jenkins? Have you ever heard of him?"

As before, she shook her head. "No, sir."

Pat sighed with resignation. "That'll be all then. Thank you for talking to me again, Cricket. You are a model of bravery, and I want you to know that I'm keeping my promise. I'm doing everything I can to find your daddy."

Cricket's composure was instantly shattered, and she began to cry, triggering Fern to hold and console her. Seeing her child so miserable brought tears to her own eyes, but she was powerless to relieve Cricket's anguish.

"I need to speak with your mother now." Pat also appeared to be affected by Cricket's disconsolation. "Would you please have a seat outside in the hallway?"

The tears continued to flow as she nodded. Fern released her and watched Cricket slowly leave the room and close the door. Such a vision made it impossible for Fern to be concerned about herself. More than anything, she wanted to follow Cricket and rock her in her arms as though she were an infant. Despite her age, Cricket was still Fern's baby, and her maternal insides were coming undone.

Meanwhile, Consuela was overtly annoyed with Pat. "It's about time that you gave B.J. the attention he's owed."

"I already told you that we were looking for him."

"Not very hard, from what I've gathered. I understand from Jasmine that you called him a phantom just yesterday."

"That can't be true." Fern promptly switched from being heartbroken to incensed.

"It was just a slip of the tongue."

"A Freudian slip." Consuela stared him down. "So you found out that his full name is Boone Jenkins?"

"That's right. We received a tip and have reason to believe that B.J. and Boone are one and the same man. But we're still investigating."

"That's better than what you've been doing, which is nothing. I'm not going to beat around the bush with you. This meeting will be the first and last time that I agree to Fern answering any more of your questions. It is clear to me that you've had one agenda, and that is to lock up my clients regardless of your lack of evidence against them. I'll remind you that neither Fern nor Hiram is your piñata, and yet—being the good people that they are—they've attempted to cooperate with your investigation only to be accused of murder during the most tragic circumstances that their family has ever faced. It all ends here, today. After we walk out of the door, you will be denied all access to my clients. Are we clear?"

The guilt on Pat's face spoke volumes. But as he shrank, Fern's faith in her attorney soared. Never had she seen a woman take command of a situation with such mastery. Without knowing it, Consuela had just demonstrated what Fern had failed to do for most of her life, to stand her ground without compromise. She remained silent, now understanding why Consuela had said that she had nothing to fear from Pat.

"I hear what you're saying, Consuela, but we'll have to see how things pan out." His gaze fell on Fern. "I know that you've been under considerable stress and you don't want to talk to me. Honestly, I can't say that I blame you. But disappearances always raise a lot of questions, and sometimes those questions bring out people's dirty laundry. You're not the first person who's been offended by me digging into their lives, but it's not personal. I'm just doing what I'm paid to do."

"Would you get on with it?"

Consuela was starkly unimpressed with Pat's speech as Fern crossed her arms without responding. She would be saying as little as possible, intending to give him nothing that he could twist around on her.

"Sure thing. I went by the hospital this morning and saw Roy. Did you hear what happened to him?"

"Yes, Consuela told me."

"He's in really bad shape, not doing well at all. Broken bones, internal bleeding. And Maggie...well, she's all torn up about it as any mother would be. I'm sure you can relate to that. I saw how you could barely hold yourself together when Cricket cried."

"Of course I can relate to Maggie."

"What's your question, Pat?"

"My question is why were you at Roy's house yesterday?"

Fern's spirits sank. She wanted to deny that she'd been there since it was her word against Roy's, but the truth would eventually come out. It nearly always did.

"Don't answer that question," Consuela counseled, but Fern had already decided to be upfront with Pat.

"It's okay, Consuela." She heaved a heavy breath. "I went there because I wanted to know where Woody is hiding. I think that he, Calvin, and Roy were into something with those phony drugs and now B.J. is in town because he got the short end of the stick."

"So you went to Roy's house after I saw you and asked you to leave?"

"That's right."

"He wasn't injured when I left. What happened between the two of you that put him in the hospital?"

"Fern, do not, I repeat, do not answer that question." Consuela's agitation was becoming more pronounced.

"Consuela, I'm sorry that I didn't tell you about going to Roy's house. But I swear that all we did was talk and he was perfectly fine when I left."

"Did he tell you where to find Woody?" Pat leaned in closer.

"No, he said that Woody is dead and I killed him." Fern threw her hands up in the air. "He wants me and everyone else to believe that Woody is never coming back."

"But you don't believe him?"

"I've already told you what I believe. Woody is hiding from B.J., and he ain't coming back home until B.J. is gone."

"Who do you think is responsible for what happened to Roy?"

"It had to be B.J. I'm telling you, Pat, that no one who's close to Woody is safe right now. B.J. is not going to stop until he gets his hands on Woody for whatever he's done."

"What about you? You're close to Woody, and no harm has come to you."

"Thank God for that. My sister thinks that I need a gun to be on the safe side."

"That might not be a bad idea unless..." He rested his back against his chair and eyed Fern closely.

"Unless what?"

"Fern, I'm going to ask you a question, and I need for you to just tell me the God's honest truth. Let's stop all the charades and put everything on the table."

"I've been telling you truth." Fern bristled at his insinuation.

"Then tell me this. Are you having an affair with B.J.?"

"What?" Fern was shell-shocked.

"That's enough. We're leaving." Consuela stood up and reached for Fern's arm.

"Of course not! What kind of question is that?" She felt Consuela yanking her up.

"Let's go, Fern. We're finished here."

"Did you promise B.J. something in return for killing Woody?" Pat also leapt to his feet like a wild animal chasing its prey.

"Absolutely not! How could you even think such a thing?" If Pat had been within reach, Fern would've slapped him. But Consuela kept a firm grip on her while dragging her out of the building with Cricket following closely behind.

Chapter 15

Pat had gotten what he'd wanted. He'd seen the look on Fern's face when he'd asked about her relationship with B.J., and he knew that she had told him the truth. She didn't know B.J. nor had she hired him to kill Woody. But Pat was still unwilling to completely rule out her complicity in whatever had happened to him. She was the perp who made the most sense, although that sense was hanging by a thread. Over and over again, he considered the fake drugs, B.J., and Roy's assault. What, if anything, connected them? Had B.J. roughed up Roy because he was somehow involved with Woody's drug activities? Or was B.J. an innocent patsy? Until Pat could question him, he was only guessing in the dark. He had to find this man, this elusive enigma. His whole case might depend on it, especially now that Calvin had refused more conversations with Pat—not that they would have made a difference anyway. At his core, Pat felt that his only hope at getting to the truth rested with B.J., who had done a fine job of making himself scarce. To help locate him, Pat enlisted the aid of the police in

B.J.'s hometown along with every eye of his own crew. He also sent up a prayer for a little help from the Big Guy upstairs.

To say the least, Fern was livid that Pat had accused her of being a harlot, so much so that she could hardly think about anything else as she went about her duties at work. Under Bernie's watchful eye, her customers' orders were going in one ear and out the other, raising his disapproving eyebrow. If she wasn't careful, he would be sending her home again, so she had to get her act together fast. Leaning on Consuela's reassurances, she reminded herself that Pat clearly had nothing that he could use to arrest her. As proof, Fern had waltzed right into his lair and emerged unscathed. Yet he remained determined to drag her name through the mud, which burned her britches and proved once and for all that cops were pigs.

As the day wore on, dinnertime inevitably arrived and Lionel strolled in. By now, Fern had managed to calm down, but her face sagged with fatigue. "Hi there, Lionel. How are you doing?"

"The better question is how are you doing? You hanging in there, kiddo?"

"Doing my best. You know what they say—whatever doesn't kill you makes you stronger."

"If that's true, then we both should be as strong as Texas longhorns." He winked at her.

"You've got that right."

"I heard that Pat is still chasing his tail, trying to figure out what happened to Woody."

Fern huffed. "A more correct statement would be that he's still chasing me."

"Nonsense!"

"I wish. I just saw him today with Consuela, and he accused me of having an affair with that guy, B.J. He actually asked if I'd paid him to kill Woody."

"That stinkin' varmint! I've had it up to here with him." Lionel held his palm above his head. "I might go over there and give him a good talking to."

"Don't waste your time. He's got no case against me or my dad, and Consuela already took him down a notch. He won't be in my face again anytime soon."

"Well, that's good." Lionel shook his head as though baffled. "I sure would like to know what happened to Woody."

"Me, too, Lionel. Me, too."

The painkillers had done nothing to ease B.J.'s discomfort, and he was beginning to realize that he had to reevaluate his plans.

He could barely move one way or the other without lightning shooting down his spine. But his trigger finger worked as good as ever. And he could still shove the barrel of his rifle into Woody's lying mouth. The more B.J. thought about it, the more he warmed to the idea. And if the gun happened to go off, well, then providence would've had the final say.

He waited until nightfall to return to Fern's neighborhood, minimizing the risk of drawing attention to himself. Before parking, he drove past her house and was addled at seeing an old green car in the driveway. Whose car was that? Had Woody come back home, or did Fern have a visitor? Something was going on that B.J. had missed, and he was greatly annoyed by the development. He needed to know who was driving that green car. Who else was in the house? Until they came out or he went in, he could only assume.

As he pondered the implications of the car, weariness began to close in on him. And despite his good fight, Mr. Sandman won the battle. Soon he was slumped over with his head leaning against the window, deaf to the world.

After what seemed like mere seconds, the sound of squealing brakes roused him, whereupon he jerked up in search of the source. The sudden movement brought on immediate remorse because the stiffness in his back had settled like concrete. He nearly howled with agony, barely managing to straighten up in his seat. When he peered outside, he realized that a young boy was staring at him through the window. Though startled, B.J. produced a lopsided smile and waved as the boy's mother ran over, apologized for his rudeness, and hurried him away. She would undoubtedly be sounding the alarm about a strange man's presence in her community, so B.J. had to act now or lose his chance.

He started his truck and drove to Fern's house, opting to spare himself the torture of walking the short distance. This morning, Fern's car was back, and—to B.J.'s surprise—the Chevy that the daughter had been driving was still there. Even more surprising, the green car was gone. What did that mean? Did the daughter take the green car? Or was she still in the house? B.J. cursed himself for falling asleep. Yet again, he had missed something that he absolutely needed to know so that he would be properly prepared for whoever was inside. But push had come to shove, and he couldn't let uncertainty stop him. This was the moment that he'd been waiting for, and despite his affliction, he shuffled to the front door and rang the bell. Trusting his primal instincts, he knew that Fern was looking at him through the peephole, although she didn't open the door or ask why he'd returned.

"Ma'am, is Woody back yet? I really need to see him."

"Woody's not here," she responded through the door. "Leave us alone, or I'll call the police."

"There's no reason to do that. I just want to talk to him. That's all." He pressed an ear against the door to better hear what she might be doing. "Ma'am? Fern?"

She'd gone silent on him, which could only mean that she was making good on her threat. So he stood back and shot the lock off the door, causing it to fly open as she screamed.

"Get out! Get out! Oh my God!" She ran toward the back with a phone in her hands. "Help! Help! Somebody please!"

"Where is he?" B.J. hobbled after her with one hand on his spine and the other gripping his rifle.

"I already told you that he's not here. He's been gone for over a week, and I don't know where he is." She screeched into the phone receiver. "Send somebody to my house. He's going to kill me!"

"Who's driving the green car that was here last night?"

"The police are coming. They're going to be here any minute." She'd run into the kitchen and was fumbling with a bolted door when he rounded the corner.

"I'm going to ask you just one more time." He aimed the gun barrel at her head. "Who's driving the green car that was here last night. Is it Woody?"

"No!"

"Either tell me the truth or die. It's up to you."

She screamed hysterically while wheeling around to face him. She pressed her back to the door as he pulled the phone off the wall to disconnect her call.

"Who's driving that damned car?"

"My daughter. It's her car. Please, please leave my children alone. They haven't done anything to you, and neither have I." Crying uncontrollably, she slid down to the floor with her hands over her face. "Please don't hurt me."

"All I want is the money that your scum-sucking husband owes me. A thousand dollars."

"I don't know nothing about that." She folded her arms around her knees as though trying to make herself as small as possible.

"I don't believe you." B.J. continued to point his gun at her and repeated, "I want my money."

"Mister, I don't have a thousand dollars. I don't even have ten dollars. You can check my purse and my bank account. I'm telling you the truth."

"Then where is Woody?" He released the safety on the gun, resulting in an audible click that elicited another scream from Fern.

"I don't know!"

B.J. took a few steps back, where he could view the living room and a hallway that appeared to lead to bedrooms. "Who else is here?"

"Nobody."

"Then who's driving the blue car since your daughter took the green one?"

"Nobody's driving it. It belongs to my sister. She let us use it after Woody took off in my daughter's car." Mascara had run down Fern's cheeks, creating dark streaks that almost looked clownish, giving B.J. pause. The woman crouched before him was clearly willing to do whatever he told her to do. And if she had his money, she was scared enough to give it to him. He believed that. He also believed what she said, that she didn't have it. So standing here in her kitchen, making demands that couldn't be met was as stupid as stupid could be.

"Damn." He lowered his gun as Fern continued to sob. "You, ma'am, are married to the worst sonuvabitch that I've ever met. Your husband, you know what he did? He took my hard-earned money, stole it like a common thief. And somebody's got to pay for that. Somebody's got to pay."

Fern made no effort to respond while continuing to weep uncontrollably.

"Ain't nothing in my life ever come easy. Everything to my name has been earned by busting my chops. I've been scrimping and scraping since the day that I was old enough to work, and now I hafta take care of my pa, too. But that don't mean nothing to people like Woody." He scrutinized her as her bawling began to quiet down. "He never told you about me?"

"N-n-no." She slowly shook her head, still heaving and sniffling loudly.

"Well, that doesn't make any sense. You don't talk to your own husband? You live in the same house, you sleep in the same bed, and you're telling me that he never said anything about what he was doing?"

"Just because he lives here doesn't mean that we talk." Her voice trembled, but the flow of tears had slowed.

"Hmph." B.J. knew that he should leave. The police would be there at any second, and things weren't going to go in his favor. But leaving wouldn't solve anything at this point. Now that he'd broken into Fern's house, the cops would scour the countryside until they found him. So he resigned himself to his fate and slowly lowered himself into a chair, grunting with the effort. "I know that I shouldn't've come here, Fern. I'm not a foolish man. But I've been so mad that I couldn't see straight. He had no right to do what he did."

"I'm sorry." She used her apron to wipe her face. "I don't know how he took advantage of you, but I'm truly sorry that he did."

"The only thing that you're sorry about is that I came here with my gun."

"That's not true. You might find it hard to believe, but we ain't so different, you and me. He's been living off of my back for the past three years."

"You don't say. Well, that just ain't right. He doesn't have a job?"

"He did, but he quit, and ever since then I've had to work day and night to make ends meet." She lowered her legs straight out in front of her and pulled her dress down. "As far as I know, all he does is play Pokémon all day like some kind of five-year-old. I haven't had a good night's sleep in so long that I can barely think on most days. And to make matters worse, he's been sleeping with prostitutes while I kill myself to keep a roof over our heads. Woody ain't no man. He's a no-count freeloader, and I'm sorry that I married him."

B.J.'s eyes fell to his feet in his sudden shame for having terrorized this hapless woman. Had he known that she was walking in shoes that hurt worse than his own, he would've stayed away from her. "Fern, I owe you an apology. I was way out of line to force my way into your home and scare you like I did. I think that your husband deserves to burn in hell, but you—well, you're right. Me and you are boiling in the same pot. Maybe if we'd met under different circumstances, we'd be friends. And if I may be so bold, I humbly request your forgiveness." He placed the rifle butt on the floor and used the weapon as a cane to help raise himself while again grumbling in pain. "I'll go outside to wait for the police. And I want you to know that I'll gladly pay for all the damage that I've done here."

Fern hesitantly rose to her feet, sticking close to the wall while watching him. "What's wrong with you?"

"My back." He grimaced. "It's gone out."

"Then maybe—maybe you should sit back down."

"No, ma'am. I've caused you enough trouble."

"There's no denying that, but—" She sighed and slowly approached him. "I don't approve of what Woody has done to you, to me, and half the town. I'm not excusing what you've done either, but there's a lot of people round here who've thought about killing him, including me." She pursed her lips. "Some people in town are saying that I already did."

"You? Aw, I don't believe that."

"Unfortunately, your opinion doesn't hold water in these parts. And you've shown that you're a poor judge of character. We both are." Fern frowned as the police sirens came within earshot. "Go ahead and have a seat. I'll handle the police."

"You're not going to press charges?"

"I should, but no. It's like you said—we're boiling in the same pot. So I'm going to give you the second chance that I intend on having, too."

When B.J. had shown up on Fern's doorstep, she'd thought that her end was near. Her whole life had flashed before her eyes, and she'd seen a future in which her children were left without her. In that moment, her survival had become her first priority. And she would've said or done anything to accomplish that objective. But things had taken a turn that she never could have expected. While listening to B.J. describe himself and his life, she'd realized that she'd come face-to-face with someone much like herself, someone whose trust had been ruthlessly abused. But unlike her, B.J. had made a choice to do something about it. He wasn't going to lie down and allow himself to be treated like a doormat. Instead, he'd decided that the wrong must be righted, although his methods were morally objectionable. Fern had to ask herself why she'd taken three long years to honor her right to fair treatment in the same way. Wasn't she equally as deserving as B.J.? She'd never stopped long enough to even think about it. But that, among so many other things, was going to change. She owed much better to herself.

For now, she couldn't in good conscious punish B.J. for doing what she'd never had the guts to do. The person who needed to be flogged was hiding out somewhere—at least, that was what Fern wanted to believe. The thought that she could be wrong, that he might actually be dead, made her shudder as she rushed to the front door to intercept the police. There she found Pat and Chip on the verge of entering with their guns drawn.

"False alarm, boys! False alarm! I screwed up." Fern raised her hands as she walked outside the house.

"What do you mean 'false alarm'?" Pat lowered his gun, but he didn't holster it.

Meanwhile, Chip continued stealthily forward.

"You don't need to go in, Chip. I made a mistake. Everything's fine."

"It doesn't look like everything's fine. How'd your door get blown apart?"

"I can explain that, but you fellas need to put away your guns."

"Come out with your hands up!" Chip yelled into the house, his gun held up and ready to be fired.

"Leave him alone." Fern attempted to intervene, but Pat grabbed her arm to hold her back. "Listen, there's been a misunderstanding. I called before I realized that B.J. meant no harm to me. He's a guest in my house. There's no reason to treat him like a criminal."

"We'll decide that for ourselves." Pat's eyes were fixed on the front door when B.J. appeared with his hands in the air. "Boone Jenkins, I presume?"

B.J. nodded and squinted in the sunlight.

"Finally, my luck is changing for the better."

Chapter 16

Life had a way of dumping a person smack-dab in the middle of a four-way road with no inkling about which direction to take. All the poor shmuck knew was that the wrong choice could end up in a long walk to nowhere. Some said that this predicament served as a warning that it was time to reassess things, to cut one's losses—and maybe they were right. But Pat wasn't the type who gave up easily even when all seemed lost. And his unyielding tenacity had always been the cornerstone of his success—until now. This time was different. This time, it seemed that the answers he sought were so far out in the distance that even the smallest speck on the horizon was nothing but a mirage. Throughout the past week, he'd been misled by some such specks, and he felt like he was looking at his last hoorah in the form of B.J. More than anything, Pat wanted to believe that the man sitting across from him would have information that finally pierced the pitch-black darkness cloaking Woody's case. But his hopes were dimmed by the clear reality that B.J. had no idea where Woody might be. Had he known, he wouldn't've gone to Fern's house looking for him. So the most that Pat might pry out of him was the reason why Woody had disappeared. Perhaps—as Fern had insisted before pledging her allegiance to B.J.—he would confess that Woody had taken off to avoid his wrath. That would be something, but still not enough to bring the man home.

Like everyone, Pat was struck by B.J.'s enormous size. As they sat mano a mano in an interview room, B.J.'s body seemed to fill the entire space. At the same time, he exuded an unexpected humility, which might be his response to Pat's authority. Most people's ballooned heads burst when they were forced to come to Jesus for a reckoning. And since B.J. was facing a steep price for his actions, Pat, at that moment, was as good as Jesus. But he wasn't interested in saving B.J. from his sins. On the contrary, he wanted to know all about them and—as was a lawman's prerogative—to use them against B.J. He wanted the truth, the whole truth, and nothing but the truth, or else he would book B.J. for breaking and entering into Fern's house. Although she'd chosen not to press charges, he didn't need her permission to hold B.J. accountable. And given that B.J. had raw abrasions on his hands that were consistent with fighting, it seemed that he needed to be held accountable for something—something obvious like Roy's assault. So Pat would start with this incriminating coincidence and see where it got him.

"You wanna tell me how you got those wounds on your hands?"

B.J. looked at them as though he'd never seen them before. "Well, I'll be. I didn't even realize that I had 'em."

"You didn't notice those bright-red marks?"

"No, sir, I sure didn't. I get 'em all the time when I hunt and skin deer at home."

"When was the last time you skinned a deer?" B.J. looked like the type who would butcher his own kill, but Pat wasn't buying it. He also dismissed the degree of B.J.'s back pain, which he seemed to be exaggerating.

"Oh, I guess it's been about a month. But I probably got scraped up a few days ago when I cut down a tree and split some firewood."

"I see. Well, I've chopped trees and firewood myself. It's hard work."

"That it is." B.J. nodded in agreement while sliding his hands under the table and out of sight.

"But it doesn't cause scratches like the ones you've got. I only see scratches like yours on people who've been fighting."

"Whoa, Nelly!" B.J. fell backward in his chair as though punched in the face. "You are sorely mistaken."

"One of the citizens in town was roughed up by someone matching your description, and I think that you did it."

"Then you'd better think again because it wasn't me." B.J. crossed his arms. "No, sir, not at all. I can barely stand up straight much less whip somebody. You've got the wrong man."

"Your back may be bothering you now, but it wasn't a problem when you chopped down that tree."

"True, but I don't have any beefs with anybody. So if that's what you heard, then you heard wrong. I'd like to know who's feeding you that garbage."

"My victim, Roy Gerritson. He says that you put him in the hospital where he is now."

"I don't know nobody named Roy Gerritson. Either he's lying or he's brain damaged, because it wasn't me who did whatever somebody did to him. No, sir, nohow."

Pat wordlessly eyed B.J. for an extended period, considering his options. Truth be told, he had nowhere else to go with this line of questions. Since Roy was claiming a total memory lapse and B.J. was standing firm in his crock, Pat was effectively beating a dead horse. Rather than waste more time, he decided to move on to more fertile ground. "I understand from Fern that you went to her home earlier this week to see Woody. Did he invite you over for a visit?"

"No, I just thought it'd be nice to look him up while I'm here."

"And why are you here?"

"I was passing through on my way to Mexico." He frowned and shook his head. "Damned shame that nobody knows where he is. When I heard the news, I thought he must be there gambling."

This was the first that Pat had heard about Woody gambling, which opened up yet another Pandora's box. "How often does he go to Mexico?"

"I don't know, but he likes to gamble when he's there, same as me."

"So you met him in Mexico while you were gambling?"

"No, I met him one night when he was stranded on the side of the road with a flat tire. He needed a jack, so I let him use mine, and we got to talking while he fixed the tire. He said that he liked to gamble on video games, and I told him that I prefer the slots. I don't have his stomach for big risks."

"When was that?"

B.J. looked upward at the ceiling, a forewarning that nothing remotely resembling facts would be coming from his piehole. "I can't recall the exact date. Could've been three months ago."

"Have you seen him since then?"

"Can't say that I have." B.J. shifted his cap, once more alerting Pat that his tongue was forked. "We ain't like kissing cousins, Sheriff. And he ain't in my back pocket."

"Woody's wife thinks that you came to Luna to settle a score with him. Is that true?"

"Of course not! I hardly know the man."

"So you didn't have any disagreements with Woody before you came to Luna?"

"Never a one. You can't disagree with someone you don't talk to."

Pat was sure that B.J. was lying. Frustrated, he pointed an accusing finger at B.J. "Then why did you blow a hole through Fern's door? Did you go there looking for drugs?"

"Huh? Drugs? You mean like the Advil in my truck? I bought those at Walgreens yesterday."

"I'm not talking about Advil. I'm talking about PCP."

"What's that got to do with me?"

"It explains why you'd do something stupid like shoot your way into someone's house!"

"Sheriff, you must be hard of hearing. I keep telling you that my back is in bad shape, and I lost my balance right after I rang the doorbell. I had the gun in my hand when I fell forward, and it just went off. It was the nuttiest thing. I can only thank the good lord that no one was hurt."

"You really expect me to believe that? Do I look like an idiot to you?"

"I know it sounds crazy, but it's the truth. I'd swear it on a stack of Bibles."

"Why'd you bring the gun in the first place? Tell me that."

"I take it everywhere in the back of my truck."

"But why'd you take it to Fern's front door? You must've had intentions to use it on somebody."

"No, sir, you're wrong again. I brought it because I thought that Woody might like to see it. I was going to try to talk him into coming with me on a hunting trip."

"Did he tell you that he'd like to go hunting?"

"No, but it wouldn't hurt to ask. I don't have a lot of friends, and he seemed nice enough." B.J. tsked. "I'm real sorry that he's missing. Real, real sorry."

"And I'm sorry that you keep peeing on my leg."

"I wouldn't do that."

Pat pounded the table and used his most menacing voice. "I know how many beans make five, and I know a liar when I see one. Now either you come clean right now, or I'm going to lock you up for breaking and entering and—by your own admission—the reckless discharge of a deadly weapon."

"I've already told you the honest to God truth, Sheriff."

"You wouldn't know the truth if it bit you on the ass."

"If that's what you think, then talk to Fern, why dontcha? Take her word since you won't take mine."

"Don't tell me how to do my job," Pat sneered. "Get up. You're coming with me."

"Where to?"

"The tank."

"You've got no cause to do that."

For the first time, B.J.'s temper flared, and Pat saw the real man, the one that had scared Fern enough to report him a few days ago. But what he couldn't see was why she'd done an about-face and decided to protect him. Had he promised her something? Were they in cahoots? At this rate, Pat might never know, and this made him even angrier, not only at B.J. but at the whole town. It felt like every resident was in on a secret that no one wanted him to know. By all appearances, they'd made a collective agreement to keep their mouths closed, which in effect had tied Pat's hands. Why would they do that? He could think of only one answer—they were glad that Woody was gone. There was no other explanation.

After ushering B.J. to a jail cell, Pat stood in his office and stared at the desk, which was annoyingly organized like it always was. At a time when he'd been busy with one of his toughest cases, the surface was clear of paperwork that suggested progress. Pat realized that this neatness might reflect a reality that he'd stubbornly ignored—that there was no case to solve. Woody was a grown man who'd lately been given to shameless self-centeredness. And it was entirely possible that he'd voluntarily abandoned all of his responsibilities. People did it all the time.

To further explore this angle, Pat placed a call to Consuela and requested Fern's confirmation of whether Woody had a passport. During their conversation, Consuela reiterated Fern's choice not to press charges against B.J., ruffling Pat's feathers yet again. An hour later, she called back with the answer that he'd expected—no, Woody didn't have a passport. But this didn't mean that he hadn't crossed the border to Mexico. Everyone knew that a little cash went a long way with the agents, who commonly accepted bribes to wave people through, no questions asked. Still, if Woody had gone to Mexico, how had Cricket's car wound up at the warehouse? And whose fingerprint had been left on the rearview mirror? These things still couldn't be explained. Nor had Pat figured out what in God's name Woody had been doing with those pills.

"Damn it to hell!"

Pat shuffled to his window and peered out at the town, the buildings, the people within view. Everything looked normal. Life was going on like nothing had happened—and perhaps that was all that Pat would ever be sure of. "Where are you, Woody Walker? Where are you?"

Two more days passed with no word from Woody, and Fern was starting to get used to the idea that he might be gone for good. While she still didn't know the details about his fallout with B.J., she'd seen enough to decide that B.J. was all right in her book. Shortly after Pat had released him, B.J. had kept his promise to pay for all the damage he'd done to her house, putting fifteen hundred smackeroos in her hand. It was more money than she'd ever seen at once and affirmed her decision to let him go free.

Courtesy of her neighbors, she had a new front door that put the old one to shame. As they always did, the community had come together when one of its own was in a bind. And though no one had said it, Fern got the impression that she would be seeing a lot more of them now that Woody was gone. If not for her children's grief, she'd wish that he stayed gone. But their long faces tempered her apathy, and for their sake she continued to hope for his return.

People commonly said that everything happened for a reason. And in Fern's view, the reason for Woody's disappearance had been to wake her up. From now on, she was going to start placing a premium on her happiness instead of putting everyone else's wellbeing ahead of her own, especially when such selflessness was ill-starred. She was also going to lose the weight that she'd gained while shouldering the whole load of her household. A new day had dawned, and a new woman had taken her head out of the sand to greet it. But before she ventured into her remade life, she was going to sleep long and hard, free from fear about what tomorrow might bring—and free from the infernal sound of Pokémon video games on the other side of her bedroom wall.

Epilogue

The seats in Cricket's car were as comfortable as bricks, not ideal for long trips. Within minutes of leaving the football game, Woody's rear was in agony, but fleeing Luna wasn't an option. He had to avoid B.J. at all costs. What was supposed to have been an easy con had turned into a full-blown crisis. And without B.J.'s money, a fast getaway would probably save his life. But that was just the beginning of his troubles. In addition to B.J.'s vendetta, he'd pissed off Shasta, and now she'd put a hex on him. While he didn't necessarily believe in voodoo, there seemed to be something to it because everything that could go wrong had gone wrong ever since he'd sold her dog to the highest bidder. Not only had she threatened to kill him, but she'd been stalking him in his dreams. Even now, he could see her holding up a chicken and slitting its neck with a blade that was almost as long as her arm. Scared out of his wits, he wouldn't be going back to Luna unless he had the means to settle both squabbles.

He glanced at the gas gauge. As expected, the tank was a little more than half-full. Cricket was always so diligent about that, such a responsible girl. She was the best thing that had ever happened to him. Because of her, he had a car to use for tonight's drive to Mexico. Who'da thought that by giving life to someone, he'd be saving his own life years later? It was a deep notion, too deep for him to dwell on, but one thing was clear—he owed her a debt of gratitude when he got back. For now, his primary focus had to be on getting out of town and checking into the hotel room that Roy had reserved for him. Once there, he would ramp up Calvin's golden idea, the product of which was in a shoebox beside him. Using Tylenol Cold and Flu capsules, Woody had made a batch of pills that he could pass off as steroids, a hot commodity among bodybuilders. If all went well, he'd be bathing in enough cash to solve his problems. And by the time his brainless buyers realized that they'd been snookered, he would be long gone.

Buoyed by his prospects, he decided to make a quick stop for a shot of genuine Mexican tequila. After showing his fake passport to cross the border, he parked in a zone that didn't require a car permit. Then, lured by the aroma of pan-fried food, he walked to a nearby restaurant that was filled with young American patrons. The atmosphere was electric, and the drinks were flowing, heightening his urge to quench his thirst. He took a seat at the bar and placed his order.

While he waited, a man sat on a stool beside him and flashed a set of brilliant white teeth. Wearing a cowboy hat and boots, he appeared to be a native Texan. "Well, look who's risen from the dead."

Woody was confused. "Uh, I think you've mistaken me for someone else."

"What?" The man slapped the bar with his palm, threw his head back, and laughed loudly. "You don't remember me?"

"I've never seen you before in my life."

"Sure you have!" Still smiling, he gazed at Woody as though waiting to be recognized, but his wait was in vain. "You really don't remember me?"

"No, I don't."

The bartender placed Woody's drink in front of him, but before he could reach for it, the man held out his hand.

"I'm Nash. And your name is Woody."

Woody hesitantly shook his hand, not sure of how to read him but beginning to feel uncomfortable.

"I'm the guy you sold a bag of bud to when I was at the bowling alley in Luna a few years ago. Remember me now?"

Woody nervously removed his hand from Nash's tight grip, vaguely recalling his face. "I don't sell marijuana."

"Well, you did that night. At least, that's what you told me. You said that it was good shit, and I said that I wanted it." He slapped the bar again, this time with a more sinister smile. "I gave you good money, and you sold me slop. Made me look like a fool to my friends. That wasn't very nice of you."

Woody remembered him now. And he sensed that the smile on Nash's face was akin to a rattlesnake shaking its tail. "I-I'm sorry. That was an honest mix-up." He reached into his pocket for his wallet. "Let me pay you back. I have some money—"

"I wouldn't hear of it." Nash held up his hand. "Mistakes happen, right?"

"Yeah, but—look, I'm really sorry. If I'd known that I'd given you the wrong bag, we could've handled it right then and there."

"We sure could've. No doubt about that."

Woody still didn't like the vibe that Nash was giving him, so he decided to cut their conversation short. "If you'll excuse me, I've gotta milk the lizard." He scooted off of his stool, intending to make a mad dash from the restaurant.

"That'll have to wait." Nash abruptly pulled out a gun and pointed it at Woody's stomach.

Frightened, he reflexively threw up both of his hands. "B-but—I thought that we were square!"

"Where'd you get an idea like that? Turn around and start walking to the door, or I'll shoot you where you stand."

"Please, please don't! Please."

In response, Nash shoved the gun's barrel deep into a fold of skin above Woody's belly.

"I'll pay you back. For the love of God, give me a chance. Don't do this."

"You're gonna pay me back, all right, but not with your money. You're gonna pay me with your work."

"W-what kind of work?"

"The kind that'll teach you not to fuck with someone who'll fuck you back. I'm putting you in the poppy fields."

"P-p-poppy fields? You mean opium? No! No, I can't do that."

"Shut up and walk!" Nash again pressed the barrel into his skin.

A cold sweat broke out on Woody's forehead, and his bladder threatened to explode at any moment. As he helplessly complied with Nash's order, his eyes darted in every direction for an escape, knowing that if he yelled, he would be killed on the spot. He was going to have to make a run for it. When they were footsteps from the exit, he seized his chance and shoved a woman into Nash before running as fast as he could, knocking bystanders out of his way. Then he slammed into a man-beast who abruptly blocked the door. Crazed with terror, Woody fell backward and hit the floor, thinking that someone in the crowd would come to his rescue, but everyone turned a blind eye.

The man-beast yanked Woody to his feet and forced him outside to a waiting car, whereupon Woody began to wail.

"Please, I'm begging you to let me go. I have a family. I have a wife and children who need me."

Nash placed his hand on top of Woody's head and pushed him down into the car.

"I don't deserve this. It was an honest mistake." Seemingly out of nowhere, he was silenced by a punch that caused him to lose consciousness.

In the ensuing haze, a tunnel appeared, and Woody gratefully floated toward it, the exit that he'd been denied at the restaurant mere moments ago. Assuming that he was dead, he expected to see the bright light that he'd heard about from those who'd died and been brought back to life. As he glided toward certain splendor, all of his earthly concerns fell away. Into the tunnel he went while slowly swaying to and fro, thanking God for his miraculous deliverance. Then something shifted, and he began to feel like he was falling and spinning out of control. Terrified, he screamed at the top of his lungs, fearful that he was on his way to hell instead of heaven. Round and round he spun with no idea which direction he was going. And then just as quickly, everything stopped. He was surrounded by dead silence, alone and trapped in a tube of nothingness. Suddenly, a white blob appeared at the other end of the tunnel and began to roll toward him as a wicked cackle echoed all around. He knew that cackle, and he knew what it meant.

Shasta had found him. She was the blob, and she'd come to take her revenge.

The amorphous object rolled to a stop in front of him, whereupon a brown iris bubbled to its surface, making Woody nauseous. Just as he knew Shasta's cackle, he knew her eyes. And the spiteful witch had transformed the blob into a giant eyeball, through which she peered at him with undisguised delight. "You ain't dead, but you're going to wish that you were. I told you that you'd be sorry for stealing my dog, you good-for-nothing asshole. Payback's a bitch."

"Don't do this to me, Shasta. I'm sorry, and I'll do anything you want. Anything." Woody tried to bow to the eye, but—did he even have a head?

"You weren't sorry until you realized that you'd messed with the wrong woman. Now your ass is mine." More evil laughter reverberated throughout the tunnel.

"Please! How can I make it up to you? There's gotta be something that I can do, something that you want."

"All I want is for you to suffer the way that I suffered when you stole my precious Pudding. And since working is your idea of suffering, you're gonna be working from sunup to sundown."

"No! I'm sorry, I'm sorry." He cried helplessly.

"Sorry won't help you this time. You're going to get what you deserve, and nobody can save you. Ya hear me? Nobody.

Your days of lying and conniving are over." The eye began to rotate, spinning faster and faster until it burst into hundreds of sparks that flickered out, leaving Woody in absolute darkness. Desolate and petrified, he let out another scream.

Jared was outside the diner smoking a cigarette when he saw Cricket's car zoom by. As it passed under the streetlights, the unmistakable shape of Woody's fat head instantly drew his ire. "Gotdamn bastard." He was barreling toward Mexico, and there wasn't one good thing that would come of it.

Shaking his head, Jared snuffed out the cigarette and returned to his job, feeling sorry for Fern. She'd really gotten a bad deal in her marriage. Yet she'd stayed, giving everyone the impression that nothing would ever change—until Woody was reported missing. At the news, the town erupted in an uproar, as most assumed that Fern had finally snapped. Even close friends like Jared doubted her innocence. He'd seen her face when she'd threatened Woody the other night. And though he was shocked that she'd done the unthinkable, she'd had the motive and the opportunity.

Pitiless speculations about Woody's fate spread faster than bed bugs. While everyone was satisfied that he'd finally gotten his comeuppance, no one wanted Fern to take the fall. She'd long been one of the town's favorite daughters, and Woody had only gotten what he'd had coming. So when she became Pat's primary person of interest, all hell broke loose. Schemes to derail his case were hatched as wild conspiracy theories abounded. But their best chance at clouding his course came when Cricket's car was spotted in the Mexico border zone. Assuming that Woody had parked it there, it seemed logical that his remains were somewhere nearby. And any numskull could do the math—if Pat got the body, Fern's goose would be cooked. The only way to avert this miscarriage of justice was to prevent him from setting his sights on Mexico. Already, the King of Kings had helped this cause by concealing Woody's body. But His flock had one more trick up its sleeve to keep Fern out of Pat's clutches. To that end, Lionel pitched a peculiar plan to Jared.

"Whaddya say we go to Mexico and bring Cricket's car back across the border?"

Bewildered, Jared's face scrunched up. "Why would you want to do that?"

"So that whatever happened in Mexico stays in Mexico."

"Ohhh." Jared leaned over and lowered his voice to a whisper. "But what if somebody finds his—" He stopped short and looked around to make sure that no one was within earshot. "Him."

"I already thought about that, and it won't matter. If the car is found in Texas but the body is found in Mexico, it'll be anyone's guess how they got split up. Pat won't know what to think."

"Uh-huh, yeah, yeah...I can see how that would make it hard for him." On the fence, Jared mulled Lionel's proposal. "He probably won't even look in Mexico unless he knows that Woody is there."

"Bingo. Now we're cooking with grease."

Still uncertain, Jared excused himself to take care of a customer, using the time to consider the idea before returning to their conversation. "I don't know, Lionel. I understand what you're trying to do, but—I don't know. What if we get caught?"

"Whose gonna tell? I don't know a single soul who's going to help Pat close his case against Fern."

"That's true. I don't either."

"Then how 'bout it? Are you in?"

Jared continued to hesitate, worried that something would go wrong. But then he thought about his devotion to Fern. She'd always been like a sister to him. And she'd never let him down when he'd needed her. This was a rare opportunity for him to repay her. "Yeah." He exhaled a shaky breath. "I'll do it."

"Good. We have to make it snappy before Pat finds out where the car is."

"Then—" He sighed again, already anxious about what lay ahead. "Let's go tonight after I get off of work."

"I was hoping that you'd say that."

They agreed to meet behind the diner, where Jared and his boyfriend, Tony, hopped into Lionel's truck. Together they rode in silence to Mexico, their mission clear. But while Lionel seemed calm and collected, Jared was agitated. He'd always been on the right side of the law, and stealing a car was unmitigated defiance. Throughout the trip, he thought about backing out. But the next thought of Fern being put in jail resurrected his resolve. For comfort, he held Tony's hand, grateful that his partner had agreed to join in tonight's caper. Without his support, Jared's knees would've buckled.

Once they reached Cricket's car, the two began the work of hot-wiring it while Lionel waited in his truck. Since neither of them had ever performed the task, they struggled for nearly an hour, during which Jared's nerves were further shredded like cheese. Finally, the engine roared to life, and Tony got behind the wheel. Then they followed Lionel back across the border and parked the car at the old Coors warehouse. Careful to cover their tracks, they wiped off their fingerprints, unknowingly neglecting one on the rearview mirror. Before locking up, Tony checked a shoebox that Woody seemed to have left behind. It was filled to the brim with yellow pills.

"What do you think these are?" He handed the box to Jared, who was breathing easier now that the deed was done.

"Hmph. Fern said that Sheriff Pat had found some drugs under her bed. These look similar to the pills that she described."

"Does anyone know what they are or what he was doing with them?"

Jared shrugged and replaced the lid. "Not as far as I know. She said that the Sheriff is getting them analyzed."

"Hmm. What if everyone is wrong about Fern? Woody could be alive and high as a kite somewhere."

"Naw, I don't think so. And these pills prove it." They walked toward Lionel's truck. "If Woody was alive, drug addict or not, I guarantee you that he wouldn't've left these behind. I'll throw 'em out somewhere on our way back home."

The poppy fields resembled a sea of red dots on the mountain where Woody worked in the scorching heat. Though only three days had passed since his abduction, the relentless slog had already caused significant weight loss. His pants sagged, and he was tired enough to sleep while standing up. But he and the other laborers knew better than to stop without their overseers' permission. They'd all seen the severe consequences for disobedience. So Woody did as told, kept his head down, and, from time to time, cried too quietly for anyone to hear him.

He had no way of proving that Shasta had cast a spell that had led to his miserable circumstances. No one would believe him, and he hardly believed it himself. Yet as she had foretold, he was working from sunup to sundown, and at this rate it would be a miracle if he didn't die from exhaustion. In his darkest hours, he clung to the memories of his family and promised himself that he'd find a way back to America, back to them. Although he saw no way to escape, he had to believe in something.

He rued the day that he'd met Nash at the bowling alley. And he bashed Shasta for ruining his life, the thought of which reduced him to tears yet again. The harder he toiled, the more he realized that he'd taken his life with Fern for granted. Indeed, he owed her one hell of an apology. If he was fortunate enough to be reunited with her, he'd be a changed man. He would beg for her forgiveness and rise to his responsibilities.

As he envisioned her face, he thought to himself, "Please, God, please help me get out of this, and I swear that I'll do whatever she wants me to do. I'll cook, I'll clean, I'll take the kids wherever they need to go. And I give You my word that I will get a job!"

About the Author

I have a passion for books, both as a reader and a writer. While I've written novels in a variety of genres, my favorite has been mystery for many years. I love to create characters and plots that keep readers guessing. I also like to defy norms and don't shy from creating highly flawed main characters that challenge socially acceptable morals and values.

I'm a native Texan and have three dogs that I absolutely adore. And I spend most of my spare time either outside with them or pursuing my other passion projects.

For information about my other novels, please visit my website: www.krysbatts.com

Made in the USA
Middletown, DE
08 July 2024